P9-DCO-137

THE rosemary spell

THE rosemary spell

VIRGINIA ZIMMERMAN

CLARION BOOKS
Houghton Mifflin Harcourt
Boston • New York

Clarion Books
215 Park Avenue South
New York, New York 10003

Clarion Books is an imprint of Houghton Mifflin Harcourt Publishing Company.
www.hmhco.com
The text was set in Berling.
Library of Congress Cataloging-in-Publication Data
Zimmerman, Virginia.
The rosemary spell / Virginia Zimmerman.
pages cm
Summary: "Best friends Rosie and Adam find an old, magical book that has the power to make people vanish, even from memory. When Adam's older sister, Shelby, disappears, they struggle to retain their memories of her as they race against time to bring her back from the void, risking their own lives in the process"—Provided by publisher.
Includes bibliographical references.
ISBN 978-0-544-44537-6 (hardback)
[1. Magic—Fiction. 2. Adventure and adventurers—Fiction. 3. Memory—Fiction. 4. Friendship—Fiction.] I. Title.
PZ7.1.Z57Ro 2015
[Fic]—dc23
2015001343
Manufactured in the United States of America
DOC 10 9 8 7 6 5 4 3 2 1
4500563958

For Kristen

One

FOR TEN YEARS, my father's furniture and books lurked in the study he abandoned. I don't remember a time when we thought he might come back, but his belongings were like a bookmark, holding a place in our lives, until Mom found out he'd moved to London. She decided to reclaim the place his absence had haunted all these years. In that brisk, decisive way of hers, she said, "Well, that's that. The room is yours, Rosemary, if you want it."

Of course I wanted it. It was twice the size of my old room, with three big windows that looked out on the river. Mom made phone calls, and men stomped up and down the stairs, and tape squawked out of its dispenser and over boxes. Then my father's possessions were gone, replaced by my bedroom furniture, its bright colors catching light that hadn't found this room for a long time. The big second-floor room at the front of the house was mine.

After the movers got the heavy stuff in place, Adam and Shelby came over to help lug armfuls of my life down the hall.

Adam kept pausing to reorganize my boxes. "Why would you put socks and colored pencils together?"

"I was just trying to make it easier to carry stuff."

He snatched the pencils from the box.

Shelby chattered easily about this book and that one. "Oh, I remember when we all read this." She pointed her chin at the battered book on top of the tottering stack she was carrying. "Don't you? It was summer, and Adam thought it would be boring and didn't want to read it, but then he did, and he couldn't put it down, and then we all read it again. And a third time, I think."

"I didn't think it would be boring!" Adam was sitting on the floor refolding my shirts.

"You did!" I remembered. "You didn't want to read a book with an old guy on the cover."

Shelby set the books on the floor between my bed and a broad bookcase, the only piece of my father's furniture I had kept. The stack slumped against the wall, the familiar covers fanned out in a welcoming display.

We must have done stuff other than read and reread that book, but when I reach into my memory, the book frames the hot, lazy months of that summer, the first one when Shelby was old enough to be responsible for us and we didn't have adults trailing us everywhere. Adam and I were nine, so Shelby was twelve, a year younger than we are now.

Adam squared a box of school supplies against the edge of the desk. "I didn't have a problem with the old guy. I just wanted to read different stuff from Shelby."

"Michelle," Shelby corrected, pulling her long hair into a messy knot on top of her head, which made her look older. She'd lately been insisting we use her full name. "It really is a great room," she said, but her attention was on her phone, and her thumbs flew as she texted.

I was suddenly exhausted. "Now that everything's here, we can set it up tomorrow," I said. "If you want to come back."

Shelby stretched, her side arcing in a graceful curve. "I think I'm going to a movie with some people . . ."

I wondered if "some people" was John, but it would have been weird to ask. A stabby ache filled in the space where Shelby used to be when it was the three of us all the time, before Shelby, or Michelle, was always busy with John or Pam and Maria or people I didn't even know.

Shelby called one of her friends as she and Adam started down the stairs, and annoyance flicked across his face, but by the time they got to the front door, he was listing his ideas for how to organize my stuff. Shelby was changing, but Adam remained the same as when we were little and he always wanted to sort Legos—not build anything, just sort them by size or color or whatever. As they stepped out into the crisp December twilight, I knew he was mentally categorizing all my things into the color-coded bins that live in his head.

So now I lean against the door frame, waiting for Adam, not quite letting myself hope that Shelby will come too. I've put away my books and most of my clothes, but I can't face doing any more on my own. Something inside me tries to shuffle out of the way so I can feel at home here, but the room isn't mine. Not yet.

Now that most of my dad's stuff is gone, I miss it. I really only know him through the things he left behind. He liked a big, heavy desk, and he kept a lot of books from English classes in college, and he put up a big copy of that annoying Escher print with the stairs that go around and around forever. Those things defined him once, giving me something to latch on to. But now I understand that those are the things he didn't care enough about to take with him.

He probably has a new desk and new books now. Maybe even a new copy of the print. Maybe he gets a new one every time he moves. Endless copies of endless stairs.

I wasn't sorry to see the print tossed into the charity truck, which was overflowing with naked baby dolls and sagging couches. My father's well-made Scandinavian desk looked sad and exposed in that truck.

Then there were the books. A battered hardcover *Norton Anthology of English Literature* with thin, translucent pages and a big, brown *Riverside Shakespeare* had stood like guards at either end of a long shelf. In between was a group of Dickens novels with black covers. Each one had a crease in the spine less than half an inch in, like he read around a hundred pages and then gave up.

I can't imagine having once loved certain books and not loving them anymore. In a way, you are what you read, so abandoning books is the same thing as abandoning a part of yourself. And the truth is that his leaving the books behind baffled me more than his leaving Mom and me behind.

So, when Mom said she'd pack up the books for the library book sale, my heart clenched, and I replied without thinking, "No. I want them," but I didn't really want them. I just wanted them to be wanted.

Now his books sit like intruders in the familiar landscape of my books. Saving them was the right thing to do, but they keep my father's absence present in the room.

Downstairs, the front door opens, and Adam calls, "Hello?"

"Come on in, you two," Mom answers. "Rosie's up in her new room."

Two?

"Thanks, Claudia."

Shelby came!

I stop myself from bounding down to the foyer. Instead, I inspect the arrangement of the furniture and hope that Adam and Shelby will help me make the room my own. My bed stretches under two windows, and my dresser sits below the third window. The huge bookcase runs all the way from the bed to the far wall, where it meets a built-in cupboard. Maybe a room is like new shoes—it'll be a little uncomfortable until I break it in.

The three of us cluster together, filling the door frame. On either side of me, their arms press into mine, like they're holding me together.

"I didn't think you were coming, Michelle." I'm careful to say Michelle instead of Shelby, even though the name is awkward in my mouth and doesn't match this person who will always, always be Shelby in my head.

She puts an arm around my shoulders. "Moving to

a new room is like graduating or getting married. It's a big deal."

"It's not that big of a deal," I murmur, but I'm glad she thinks something having to do with me is a big deal.

She glides into the room and starts rummaging through a laundry basket overflowing with stuffed animals.

I cringe and say quickly, "I meant to put those in the attic."

"Why?" Adam sounds wounded.

"They're little-kid things."

"You can't put Sheepy in the attic!" Shelby holds up a sheep that's faded from a baby pink to well-loved gray.

Of course I can't. Of course she wouldn't expect me to. Why was I even worried?

Shelby starts to arrange the animals on the dresser at the foot of my bed.

Adam cries, "You did the books without me!"

"Don't worry. We can redo them." I cross to the bookcase. "I kept some of my father's, but . . . I don't like them mixed in with mine."

He doesn't ask why. He just trots forward and starts pulling books off the shelves and piling them on my desk. He knows which ones are mine and has no trouble picking out the intruders.

Shelby kneels with her head cocked to one side, reading titles.

"I love your books," she sighs.

"That's because they're the same as yours," Adam points out.

He's right. So many of my books are ones she recommended. If you are what you read, then Shelby's been a big part of making me who I am.

"Are these organized in any way?" Adam frowns at the shelf.

"Well, they're together by author—"

"Of course."

"Yeah, and then the ones that are most important are nearest my bed at pillow level, you know, so I can get them quickly."

"In a reading emergency." Adam grins at me, but his eyes are serious. We've both experienced those times when only the right book will anchor you.

"The books on the top shelf are ones people've given me that I haven't read yet but mean to, and in between is kind of everything else. The bottom is poem books and my dictionary and atlas and stuff."

He nods. "Reference and nonfiction."

At some point in the near future, he will volunteer to make labels for my shelves, and I'll let him. It'll make him happy, and I like the idea of Adam putting his personal stamp on my room.

Shelby pulls her phone from her pocket. She leans forward, and her hair sheets across her face, so I can't see it.

"What do you want to do with these?" Adam rests a hand on the stack of my father's books.

"I don't know." I bite the inside of my lip. "It seemed wrong to give them away, but I don't exactly want to keep them, either."

I want Shelby's input, but she's texting.

"The attic?" Adam suggests.

"That seems cruel."

He frowns. "To your dad?"

"To the books."

"Sorry, guys. I've gotta go!" In a heartbeat, Shelby's up and in the doorway.

"Okay. Thanks for coming." I manage a neutral tone. Happy she was here. Fine with her leaving.

"At least I got these guys all set up." She smiles in the direction of the stuffed animals. She's not being condescending, but she's leaving to meet a boy, and I'm such a child. How can she possibly want to be my friend?

"See ya!" And she's gone.

There's a pause during which Shelby's absence is the biggest thing in the room.

"How about the cupboard?" Adam tugs me back to business.

The shallow cupboard sits expectantly in a corner space that used to be a chimney. "Okay, I guess."

Adam opens the top door. "His books will fit here, and then you'll have them, but you can close the door and, you know, out of sight out of mind, right?"

It only takes a few minutes to arrange the books in the cupboard. *The Riverside Shakespeare* leans to the left, holding the others in place.

Adam shuts the door. "There!"

He collapses into my papasan chair and surveys the scene.

I plop down on the bed and look out the window at the river racing past the island.

"Can you see Constance Brooke's house?" Adam asks.

"Yes," I answer. "And a kind of dark place that must be the rosemary patch. From here, you can see how close the rosemary is to the ruins."

In the summer, Adam and Shelby and I row to the island and climb on the broken walls. We play hide-and-seek and dig in the ruins like archaeologists. Shelby found a button once, which led to a long elaborate game about magic buttons like the ones in a book she'd recommended. In the weird light of summer evening, the magic seemed real.

Sometimes we just hang out. Adam practices lassoing with the boat rope. Shelby and I climb the V tree and lean against the strong branches and talk. It's a willow tree with smooth gray bark. We each take a big step up to plant a foot in the crevice where the trunk splits in two, and then I take the right side of the V and Shelby takes the left. In summer, the branches hang around us in light green ropes that enclose us and cocoon us. This is where she told me about *Pelagia's Boats*, and then we all read it, and it was the best book ever. Pelagia and the young king have to do their best when all the experts say everything is hopeless, and then they sail off to a new world and hope blossoms off the page. I reread the end every time I'm even slightly sad. It sits now, its spine all cracked and shredded, on the shelf right by my bed.

Now that Shelby is spending less and less time with us, how will I know what to read? Mom suggests classics, but she's too eager for me to love them. Shelby always discovered books that were just perfect. Does *Michelle* even like to read?

I turn away from the island and back to my room. It's in the old part of the house with wide floorboards and carved molding around the door and windows. All the corners and edges are muffled by layers and layers of paint. Layers and layers of people who've called this room their own.

"It was someone else's room before it was my dad's," I blurt out.

"Huh?" Adam looks at me, puzzled.

I fumble to explain. "I just mean it feels weird to take over my dad's room, but the house is two hundred years old, so it's not his room, really, in the whole big history of the house. Lots of people have lived here, like, you know, Constance Brooke."

"Sure. She lived here for seventy years or something, right? From after the flood wrecked the island house until you moved in. So it's way more her room than your dad's." He leans back against the green cushion and smiles at me. "Mr. Cates said he'd make poets of us all by the third marking period, so it's totally appropriate for you to take over a poet's room. It's passed from local poet Constance Brooke to local poet Rosemary Bennett."

"I hardly think one creative writing elective makes me a poet," I protest, but I warm to the idea that I'm somehow more connected to Cookfield's local poet than to my father.

"Every poet starts with a creative writing elective," Adam says sagely.

We digest that nugget of wisdom in silence. I sit on the bed, trying to fall in love with the room. Adam studies the space, reorganizing my stuff in his head.

"What are you going to do with the lower cupboard?" he asks.

"It doesn't open, remember?"

I have no idea what the lower cupboard contains. The small white door, maybe two feet high, has never opened.

We're both remembering that rainy day—two summers ago?—when we spent a long afternoon trying to break into the locked cupboard. Mom discovered us and said, "You know you're not supposed to play in here."

"We're not playing!" Shelby was indignant.

We were very serious about opening the door, but Mom stood watch until we shuffled out of the study. I hate the feeling of getting caught doing something bad, so when Shelby suggested we try the door another day, I deflected her.

Adam launches himself out of the low chair. "Let me just try . . ." He drops to his knees and tugs at the small metal knob, painted over many times like everything else in the room.

"We did this already," I protest. "You know it's stuck."

"We were younger then. We didn't know what we were doing," he mutters as he examines the door.

"Shelby tried to use a credit card," I remind him.

"She also tried 'Open Sesame,'" he replies.

"Neither worked."

"Well, Shelby isn't a thief or a magician," he says. "So maybe we weren't trying the right things. We just need to be systematic . . ." His tongue pokes just slightly out of the corner of his mouth, the way it does in algebra.

"It's never opened." I speak slowly, as if enunciated syllables might make him stop messing with the door.

"But that's stupid." He doesn't look at me. His back flexes as he pulls. "It's a door. It has to open. Or at least it did once, so it can . . . Or. Should. Now." He smacks the small door with each word. Nothing happens.

"Adam!" I hate when he just won't let something go. "Leave it. It doesn't matter."

He's shifted from smacking to gently twisting the knob.

"I've lived in this house my whole life." I raise my voice, trying to pull his attention away from the door. "And that cupboard has always, always been locked or stuck. Even when my father lived here, he never opened it."

"Maybe he didn't try." Adam looks up at me.

Of course he didn't try. I bite the inside of my cheek.

The overwhelming desire to not be like my father propels me across the room, and I kick the little door. Hard. I expect it to spring open, in response to my sudden fury, but nothing happens. I kick it again. And again.

Adam shifts a little to the side and waits for me to stop.

After four kicks, I'm spent. I drop to my knees and grip the knob. It moves left and right, but the door doesn't budge.

Adam leans in with me. "It's like it's locked somewhere else. You know what I mean? The knob turns, but it doesn't open the door."

"Well, there's no other handle," I sputter as I twist harder.

He reaches over me and tries to grip the edge of the door, but the crack is too small. "Do you have a crowbar?" he asks.

"I don't know. Is that something people have?"

"I think so. Usually."

"I'll get the toolbox." I push myself up, and the wide floorboard shifts underneath my hand.

Adam's eyebrows arch. We slide off the board. He presses it with the palm of his hand, and it rocks, just slightly.

"Do you think . . ." he starts.

But I'm already there. I stick a finger into the pinky-size hole where a knot used to be and lift the board. Adam grasps the end, and together we set it to the side. The space underneath is cluttered with a ragged gray cotton I recognize as the same insulation that's in the attic. Nestled in the cotton are a puzzle piece and a marble, dimmed by dust.

Adam pulls out the puzzle piece and blows it clean. "It's wood," he observes. "It has flowers or maybe leaves . . ."

I pluck it from the flat of his hand. Whatever was once pictured here has faded to an unrecognizable smudge of ferny green. I set it next to the rectangular opening in the floor and reach for the marble, which manages to glint through the dust.

"What was that book?" Adam asks. "The one where the mean mother person traps kids' souls in marbles?"

"*Coraline*," I whisper, and I dump the marble into Adam's hand.

"No souls here," he says lightly. "Just dusty glass."

Just the forgotten toy of some kid who lived in this house fifty or a hundred years ago, then grew up and grew old and probably died.

I look away from the abandoned marble to the empty space beneath my floor. Filling it will push away the creepiness, and my mind darts across my belongings, in search of items I could hide here.

Something black catches my eye. A small J-shaped piece of metal hangs down from the base of the cupboard.

I grasp the crook of the J. It's a handle. I'm sure.

Adam leans in again. "Is it—"

"Wait," I breathe.

I push the cool metal to the right. For a heartbeat, the small handle resists, and then, as if with a sigh of relief, it gives.

The cupboard door swings open.

Two

THERE'S ONE SHELF. On the shelf is a book. An old book.

A secret, ancient book! Authors I love appear in my mind. E. Nesbit leaps up and down with excitement, and J. K. Rowling raises an eyebrow.

Adam nudges me with his elbow. "Pick it up."

I lift the book. It's heavier than I expected, and I have to catch it with my left hand to keep it from thunking to the floor.

The cover feels like skin. Thick skin. A coating of dust clings to the cracked and peeling burgundy leather.

"What is it?" Adam asks, his arm pressing against mine as he leans forward.

I check the front and the back. The spine. "There's no title."

I open the cover, and a sweet, musty smell escapes. "I wonder how long since anyone touched this," I muse. "It could be fifty years or a hundred. Or more."

A forgotten toy is sad, but a forgotten book makes all sorts of promises.

"There's a name!" Adam points to the inside cover.

In the upper left corner, letters loop into each other in a slanted, old-fashioned cursive.

"Constance Brooke," Adam and I read together.

"It *was* her room!" he exclaims, shoving my shoulder for emphasis. "I told you!"

The first page is blank. I turn it, and my fingers, so familiar with books and their pages, find themselves in a foreign country. The paper is the color of sand, and it's stiff, like it got wet and then dried out.

"Do you think this is parchment?" Adam asks in a low, library voice.

"Parchment is way older than Constance. I mean, parchment is Bible old, or at least Declaration-of-Independence old."

Mom would know if this is parchment, and she could probably guess the book's age too, but I don't want her to see it and make it hers. She's always buried in books. This one is mine. Mine and Adam's.

Adam runs his fingers reverently down the page. "Shelby'd love this," he says. "What was that story you two read about the kids who find a magic book in the library?"

"*Seven-Day Magic,*" I answer, pulling my phone from my pocket. I try to call Shelby, but she doesn't pick up.

Adam shrugs. "We'll show it to her later."

I set my phone on the floor next to the book. "They're both communication devices, really," I point out. "But from different universes."

"Different times," Adam says.

"Right." I lean back. "Like Constance is from a different time than parchment. I mean, if it is parchment, then it must be hundreds of years old, so why is her name in the book?"

"Hmm," Adam begins. "If only we could find—I don't know, like, an English professor to ask . . ."

"We are not asking my mother!" I glare at him. "If this is actually really old, then she'll take it away. She'll hurry it off to the library to be preserved in a vacuum-sealed vault, and she'll organize us into little field trips to visit the book in its sterile, soulless book prison. She'll probably find some way to write an article about it too, and then it won't even be our discovery anymore. We found it. In my room. It has nothing to do with her."

He puts out his hands in an okay-okay gesture. "Fine, Rosie. Fine. We won't ask your mom."

I slide my fingers under the next page and lift it, using only the pads of my fingers and the gentlest movement. Mom's not the only one who can treat an old book with care. It has to be parchment. It's heavy in a different way than paper.

We almost miss the handwritten phrase just above the middle of the page. The ink's faded to a tea brown, only a shade darker than the parchment.

"*Diary of* . . . who? What does it say?" I pull back, the way Mom does when she's trying to read something small, but it doesn't help.

Adam runs a finger below the writing, marking each letter. "*A Poet,*" he reads. "*Diary of a Poet.*"

"It's Constance's diary!"

"This is just totally unbelievable." He thrusts his hands through his hair, making it stand up in little tufts.

"I have to try Shelby again," I say. She still doesn't pick up.

We study the old diary in awed silence. I imagine going on a talk show to describe how we made the greatest literary discovery of the twenty-first century while Mom stands in the wings, ferociously proud of me.

There's more writing on the next page. A list in two columns. The handwriting seems the same as the title but even more faded. Some items are just pale ghosts of words. Others are darker, and we take turns figuring out the loops and frills that form strange letters.

"That curl is just a decoration," I murmur. "And that funny squiggle is an *s,* I think." I point to a double letter in the middle of a word.

"Looks like an *f* to me," Adam says.

"Yeah, but look . . . that must be *sage* and so this one would be *hyssop.* That's more likely than *hyffop,* I guess, but what's hyssop?"

"No idea." Adam grabs a notebook and pencil from my desk. He makes columns, using his special power of being able to draw crazy straight lines without a ruler, and sorts the words. He copies *sage* into a column labeled "Qualities" and puts *hyssop* in the question-mark category.

The next word is *chamomile,* and Adam labels another column "Types of Tea."

"Wait." I put a hand on his arm. "Sage, hyssop, chamomile, this one's lemon balm, marjoram, right? Next is lavender. This is basil. Thyme. Mint, and—"

"Rosemary!" Adam cuts in with a smile. "They're herbs!" He pushes away the notebook. "But why? What for?"

"Maybe she was making notes for poems about herbs?" I suggest.

I turn the page.

Nothing. And more nothing.

Just blank sheets of parchment, yellowed and stiff.

Disappointment settles over me like an itchy blanket.

"Maybe she realized poems about herbs would be insanely boring," Adam suggests.

"But Constance Brooke wrote lots of poems," I protest, still turning pages, less carefully now. "I mean, even if you only count the ones we've had to read in school, that's, I don't know, twenty at least, and she won prizes and stuff. She's famous!"

Adam clasps his hands like an old-fashioned schoolboy and recites:

> Through the window poke twigs and grass
> A robin nests at my room's edge
> A wooden frame pokes in the nest
> A woman's room beyond my ledge.

I stare at him. "Why is that taking up space in your head?"

He shrugs. "It's hard to forget something once you memorize it. Like, *Four score and seven years ago*—"

I cut him off. "Maybe the diary was a present, like a blank book or a journal, you know? And she started to use it but then abandoned it."

"Maybe," he agrees. "Or maybe she found it. Maybe it belonged to someone else before it was hers." He carefully flips between the list and the inside cover. "The handwritings are different, see? Like the *s* and *f* thing. Constance has a regular *s,* not like these ones in *hyssop.*"

"So there could be two different poets." I like this idea. Layers of poets.

"You know what I think?" Adam's eyes are huge. "I think this book's been waiting for you. Constance left it in the cupboard for a future poet."

Sometimes I recognize younger Adams in his face. The one that looks at me now, all eager and earnest, is about five and sincerely believes that we can build a secret tunnel between our houses. Adam's faith that people might leave ancient books hidden in cupboards for future generations to find is infectious. I believe he could be right.

My phone buzzes loudly against the hardwood floor. Shelby!

"Hey, Rosie. You called?"

"Hi, Sh . . . Michelle." I look at Adam.

He mouths, "Cupboard."

"We got the cupboard open. You know the one in my dad's . . . in my room?"

"Really? That's great. How—Wait, hold on." A loud jumble of voices and laughter makes me pull the phone away from my ear. "Rosie? Was there anything inside? Oh, hang on again. Rosie? I'm so sorry, but I have to go. John! Yeah, I'm coming. Rosie, we'll talk later, okay? See ya."

She's gone. "Bye," I whisper to the silence.

"She'll be excited when she sees what we found," Adam says quickly. "She just doesn't get it yet."

I decide to look forward to showing Shelby the book instead of thinking about the way her call left me dangling. Adam's right. She'll be just as excited as we are once she sees it.

"You know who else would love this?" I start to shape a plan.

"Your mom?"

"Mr. Cates! We should use this for our poetry journal. For class."

Adam frowns. "But we can't write in it. It's probably valuable."

I shove away reason. "It would be in a library if it was valuable. Or a museum. Besides, it's mostly blank."

"Maybe we should ask your mom—"

"No!" I didn't mean to shout. I take a breath. "No."

Adam looks at me the same way he did three years ago when I wanted to go swimming in the river. He was right: That would have been stupid. But this is just a book. An old book, sure. But it's just paper or parchment sewed together and left in a cupboard.

I blaze ahead. "There are already two layers of people who wrote in it. That's like an invitation to us to be a third. What should we write? All those blank pages . . . We should use a pen . . ." I riffle through a box of desk stuff and pull out the bookmark Adam made for my birthday last month. Sprigs of rosemary from the patch on the island braided around a piece of gold ribbon and pressed flat.

When he gave it to me last month, I asked, "How'd you get the rosemary?" because we hadn't been to the island since August. The thought that maybe he and Shelby went without me made my heart squirm.

"I got it when we went in the summer," he explained. "It's taken two months just to get it so flat!" They didn't go without me. He'd been thinking about my birthday for months.

I set the rosemary in the diary, and its piney scent wafts up.

"Here's a pen." I pull one from the box. "Let's put our names."

I know we shouldn't. The diary belonged to Constance Brooke and maybe someone else before her. Mom would have a fit. Worse, she would be disappointed in me. But I write my name. Not on the parchment but on the inside cover, which is a soft, yellowed paper glued to the leather binding. It takes the ink a second to settle into the page.

Adam leans close to me and writes his first name below mine. His familiar handwriting—the way his capital *A* is super pointy at the top—reassures me.

He looks up at me. "How old do you think it is, really?" What he means is, "Are we going to get in trouble for this?"

I answer truthfully. "Old enough that my mom would completely have a seizure if she knew we were writing in it." I'm half smiling and half terrified. And also a little proud. We've marked this valuable, important, ancient book as our own. "But even though it's old, it's empty. It's just paper. Or parchment."

Adam sets his concern aside and writes his last name slowly and neatly, so now there is another list in the book: *Constance Brooke. Rosemary Bennett. Adam Steiner.*

Shelby's name should be there, too. She makes her *S*'s so that they kind of underline the rest of her name. Now that she's Michelle, I wonder if she does that somehow with the *M*.

Adam gazes at the book. He pushes his hair off his forehead again. He looks hopeful, expectant.

The book lies on the floor. The names rest on the page. Nothing happens.

"It kind of seems like an ancient, hidden book might be—I don't know," he stammers. "It ought to be, like, magic."

"You mean you thought the book would write back?" I joke, but I'm not really joking. Somewhere deep inside my imagination, I was hoping the book might be magic too.

Suddenly I'm heavy with the business of being real in a world that offers stories about wizards and spells and fantastical lands but confines all that wonder to books. I thought the diary was wonderful, but it's not. It's just old and dusty.

Deflated, we stash the book in the secret compartment under the floorboard and busy ourselves organizing my desk. The joy of sorting rescues Adam's mood, but disappointment pecks at me.

It's gotten dark, and it's almost time for dinner.

Before he goes, Adam checks his work. Like always. He pulls out each tidy desk drawer to admire his system. He found a bunch of those little boxes for jewelry in Mom's wrapping paper stash, and they're are all lined up in my drawer, one with paper clips, one with rubber bands, even a long necklace one for pencils. "You have to try to keep it like this."

"I'll try." We both know I won't succeed. I'm not exactly a slob, but organization is not high on my list of priorities. That's why I need Adam.

He echoes my thought. "I'll help you."

The doorbell rings, and Mom's clogs clomp across the floor downstairs. Adam and I stand still, listening. Could it be? Voices rise up the stairs.

"It's Shelby!" I announce, and we turn to greet her.

"Hey, I came to get you," she says to Adam. Her hair is tumbled up on top of her head again. She's wearing yoga pants, which used to mean she'd been at dance class, but she stopped taking dance.

Adam mumbles, "I can walk home by my—"

But I cut in. "You won't believe what we found in the cupboard!"

"Oh, right!" She remembers the call. "How'd you get it open?"

"There was this hidden latch," I begin, and then Adam's explanation and mine tumble over each other. We tell her about the floorboard and the J-shaped handle.

"And the door just swung open!" Adam announces.

"And?" Her hands are on her hips. "What was inside?"

Adam and I look at each other and grin.

"A book." We answer together, like a small choir. The word resonates in the room.

Shelby looks appropriately awestruck. "Wow! What book?"

"You won't even believe—" I start.

"It's really old," Adam says.

"Like, with parchment!" I add.

"And two handwritings. One is definitely ancient."

Together we remove the floorboard and set it aside. Adam steps back, and I use two hands to lift the book from the hiding space. I hold it out to Shelby.

She stares at the cracked burgundy cover, brighter

since Adam and I wiped away most of the dust. She pushes a stray lock of hair behind her ear. "It looks just like—"

"*Seven-Day Magic,*" Adam says.

"Riddle's diary from *Harry Potter,*" I say.

"Something from a book." Shelby smiles.

The three of us sit on the floor. We show Shelby where *Diary of a Poet* is written, and she leans forward to squint at the list of herbs while Adam and I translate the faded letters for her.

"But how do you know it belonged to Constance Brooke?" she asks.

I show her the inside cover.

"You wrote in it?" She is aghast.

"It's mostly all blank, so we figured . . ." Adam knows this is a lame excuse.

I go defensive. "We found it. In my room. If it was valuable, it would be locked up somewhere, so . . ."

"It was locked up here," Shelby protests, enunciating each syllable in that way adults do when you willfully misunderstand them.

I take the book from her. "Yes. Here. In *my* room."

"Your new room."

"Whatever." I shrug.

"Look." Adam tries to make peace. "It probably is old and maybe even valuable, but all that's in it is the list, so we figured Constance abandoned it."

"And someone else abandoned it even before her," I add. "So Constance double-abandoned it."

"Right," Adam agrees, relief in his voice. Even Mom might agree that a book double abandoned is fair game.

"You have to be on our side." My voice comes out in a whine. I add in a more solid tone, "It's going to be our poetry journal."

Shelby uncrosses her arms and runs her hands down her sides as if smoothing away better judgment. "Mr. Cates will love it," she concedes. "I forgot how he makes partners share a journal. 'So your ideas can stand on each other's shoulders,'" she remembers. "Come on, Adam. Mom actually cooked dinner. We need to go." As we file down the stairs, Shelby asks, "Does he still talk about the muse all the time?"

"I think Mr. Cates gets kickbacks from muses," Adam says.

Shelby laughs. "That was such an awesome class." She reaches the front door but stops. The laugh is gone. Her eyes dart from Adam to me. "Does it . . ." She stops, crosses her arms again. "Does it do anything? The book? Does the book do anything?"

Adam and I shake our heads.

"Oh, well. I mean I didn't really think . . . You put the idea in my head with *Seven-Day Magic* and whatnot." She laughs again, hollowly this time. She pulls her hair out of its clasp, and it sheets down her back. She and Adam disappear down the street.

I stand alone in the foyer. The air shivers with the question. Does the book do anything? To even ask that . . . in real life . . . and Shelby asked it . . . The air shimmers with possibility. Joy swallows me whole.

Three

WE HAVE CREATIVE WRITING TODAY, so I have the diary in my backpack. It waits under my seat during Spanish, where we practice the verb *escribir,* "to write." *Escribo. Escribes. Escribe.* Shelby said Spanish was better than French because the teacher was more fun and did all sorts of cool games to help learn the language, but then that teacher switched to the high school. Sigh. *Escribimos.* We write.

Finally, I drop my backpack next to my seat in Mr. Cates's room. He's changed up the desks again. A couple weeks ago, they were in a big circle facing the middle of the room. That was when Mr. Cates started doing the poem of the day. The first one was by Emily Dickinson and began *I dwell in Possibility.* We had to all write about what we thought that meant. Then the next day, the desks were in the same circle but all facing out, and we read this Wordsworth poem about daffodils, and we had to look inside ourselves and find a memory to write about. Last class, we were in pods of five. Today, the room is dotted with pairs of desks set side by side.

"Partner up," Mr. Cates calls, as everyone hurries into the room.

Most classes, kids kind of straggle in, but in Mr. Cates's creative writing class, everyone comes right in and sits down.

I sit near the front, and Adam slides into the seat next to me.

"Howdy, pardner," he says in a bad cowboy accent.

"Hi, Adam."

"Do you have the book?" he whispers.

I tip my head toward my backpack.

Mr. Cates perches on his desk. He runs fingers through his curly hair to get it out of his face. He adjusts his glasses. "Page one hundred seventeen, people," he says, carefully turning pages, like the book is really special, even though it's just a paperback poetry anthology.

He started the pods-of-five day with a poem by E. E. Cummings that didn't make any sense at all, but then somehow it did, and we all had to write without rules, which was surprisingly hard. Especially for Adam.

Today's poem is by Shakespeare.

"Going traditional today," Adam murmurs.

"This one will have rules," I whisper. "You'll love it."

Mr. Cates starts to read in a rich, layered voice that lifts the poem off the page and delivers it personally to each of us.

> Not marble, nor the gilded monuments
> Of princes, shall outlive this powerful rhyme . . .

"Powerful rhyme!" he repeats, and the corners of his eyes crinkle as he smiles.

> But you shall shine more bright in these contents
> Than unswept stone, besmear'd with sluttish
> time.

"Sluttish!" Josh Baum snorts.

Mr. Cates stares at Josh over his book, managing to communicate disdain without looking unkind.

"Sorry," Josh mutters.

Mr. Cates raises the book again.

> When wasteful war shall statues overturn,
> And broils root out the work of masonry,
> Nor Mars his sword nor war's quick fire shall
> burn
> The living record of your memory.

He stops. "That syntax is tricky. Let me paraphrase. Shakespeare says neither war nor ruin can destroy the record of your memory. And what's the record? Josh? Miranda?"

Miranda flips her hair. "Uh, the record is the poem? Is that right?"

"Sure is." Mr. Cates beams. "Nothing will destroy your memory because it lives forever in rhyme. This. Powerful. Rhyme. Next line."

> 'Gainst death and all-oblivious enmity

"What is 'all-oblivious enmity'?"

No one speaks up.

He prompts, "Enmity?"

"Like enemy?" Micah suggests.

Mr. Cates nods. "Yes. It's a feeling of hostility. So then, what is 'all-oblivious'? Adam?"

"Something about forgetting," he says. "Like oblivion."

"Right. So . . . forgetting is the enemy, and what defeats forgetting? Memory! Yes?" He looks around the room to make sure we're all following and continues.

> 'Gainst death and all-oblivious enmity
> Shall you pace forth; your praise shall still find
> room

Even in the eyes of all posterity
That wear this world out to the ending doom.
So, till the judgment that yourself arise,
You live in this, and dwell in lovers' eyes.

He lets the silence hang in the room before he asks the now-familiar question: "What does it mean?"

I say, "It means the person he loves will, like, live forever in the poem."

Adam adds, "And the poem lasts even when other kinds of monuments are gone."

Mr. Cates cocks his head to one side. "You said 'other kinds of monuments.' Is the poem a monument?"

Adam sits forward. "Yeah, isn't it? The poem is a way to . . . to hang on to the person, even though they're gone. That's what monuments do."

"But it's kind of dumb," says Kendall. "Monuments are, you know, stone and stuff that would totally last longer than a poem. I mean, a poem is just a piece of paper."

"Indeed," Mr. Cates replies. "If Shakespeare carved his lover's name in stone, it would certainly outlast a piece of paper."

"But paper lasts," Adam protests. He avoids looking at my backpack, and I know he's thinking about the ancient book in there.

"Yeah," Aileen chimes in. "Adam's right. I mean, look at the library. It's practically all paper."

"But it's not just the paper," I say. "It's the words. They're kind of bigger than the paper."

Mr. Cates takes a step toward me. "Go on," he prods.

"So, Shakespeare didn't write on these actual pages," I explain, and I thwack my book for emphasis. "His poem is just reprinted here and in lots of other books—"

"And it's been in print for about four hundred years, right?" Micah adds.

"Right," I agree. "So, it's the poem itself—the words, not the paper—that lasts longer than a stone."

"Nice." Mr. Cates smiles encouragement at all of us. "This. Powerful. Rhyme."

He claps his hands together. "Shakespeare—the Bard, *the* Bard—is our inspiration for today. Take out your journals. You can start with a line or two from the poem we just read, or you can use any Shakespeare lines you know . . ."

Josh cuts in. "What Shakespeare would we just know? We don't all sit around memorizing poems." He sort of laughs and looks around for support, but when it comes to giving Mr. Cates a hard time, he's on his own.

Mr. Cates puts his hands on his hips, his feet shoulder width apart, like he's about to start exercising. "What Shakespeare do you know?" he asks the room.

"To be or not to be?" Miranda offers.

"Friends, Romans, countrymen," Kendall says.

"Wherefore art thou Romeo?"

"All that glitters is not gold!"

"To thine own self be true," Aileen says. "Or is that Jesus?"

Mr. Cates laughs. "It's Shakespeare. See, Josh, most people know Shakespeare. He inhabits the English language like oxygen inhabits air. We breathe him in even when we don't know it."

The energy in the room is practically vibrating. I don't know if it's Shakespeare or Mr. Cates who's gotten us so inspired, but I can't wait to begin writing.

Mr. Cates drops his hands to his sides. "Just copy down any Shakespeare you like, and then write what comes to you."

I pull the diary from my backpack like I'm lifting a fragile, living thing. I place it on the desk between Adam and me and open to the first blank page.

I angle my hand for cursive and carefully unspool the *Hamlet* quote Mom took my name from:

There's rosemary, that's for remembrance. Pray, love, remember.

"Good choice." I hear the grin in Adam's voice.

Mr. Cates circles toward us. I take a breath. "Mr.

Cates? We found this old-looking blank book. Is it okay if Adam and I use this for our journal?"

Mr. Cates frowns ever so slightly. "It looks very old—" he begins.

"I know!" I try to strike a tone somewhere between mildly pleased and a little shallow. "Doesn't it?"

"Where did you find it?" He steps closer.

If he really sees the diary, he'll know it's not pretend old. He'll know we shouldn't be writing in it.

"Mega Mart," I lie. It's an insult to this book to even think about it and Mega Mart together.

Mr. Cates backs off. "Sure. Use whatever inspires you," and he circles on to another pair.

"So what are you inspired to write?" I ask.

"Funny," Adam says, his fingers resting lightly under the line from *Hamlet*. "You are writing about herbs, like the list."

"As you pointed out yesterday, poems about herbs would be pretty boring. How about the remembrance part?"

"Okay," Adam agrees. "That's good, since the sonnet was about memory too."

"Sonnet?"

"The powerful rhyme poem Mr. Cates just read?" Adam looks at me like I'm slow.

"He didn't say it was a sonnet."

"He didn't need to!" Adam returns. "It had three

sets of four lines and then two rhymed lines at the end. That's how sonnets work. Or at least Shakespeare's sonnets. I think there's another kind with a different structure."

"I guess I was right about you and the rules." I smile to show I think it's cool he knows this.

Adam scoots closer to the diary. "Do you have any ideas?"

I read the *Hamlet* line aloud and close my eyes, waiting for inspiration to strike.

"A blank page is an invitation," Mr. Cates intones.

Invitation. Party. Memories of parties? Inspiration isn't striking.

"Rosie." Adam's voice cracks. "Look at the page."

I follow his gaze to the blankness below the rosemary line, but it isn't blank. Faint writing trails like tendrils down the page.

Is the book finally writing back? It can't be. My brain races, trying to make sense of what I see.

Adam says in a low voice, "We didn't see it before because the ink's so light."

He's right. It's barely darker than the page itself.

I tip the book to get a better look, and for once I'm grateful for the harsh fluorescent lights in the classroom.

The letters slowly resolve into view. It's as if my eyes are adjusting to the dark, recognizing shapes where before had been nothing but grainy blackness. "Is it even English?"

"It's not the same writing as the herbs," Adam says. "It's more modern, like Constance's."

I focus on one letter at a time. "This is a *W*," I murmur, tracing the slanted cursive with my pinky nail.

"That's an *i*, and so's that." Adam points.

"*Wilkie!*" I read triumphantly.

"What's a wilkie?" Adam frowns.

"It's a name," I reply as I move on to the next word. "You know, like 'wee Willie Wilkie.'"

"It's 'wee Willie Winkie,'" he scoffs.

"Whatever. Wilkie is a name. The next word is *says*. *Wilkie says . . .*"

Adam picks up the thread. "*Wilkie says I should . . .*"

"*I should write down . . .*" I continue.

"*Write down my thoughts . . .*" Adam stops.

"*If I want to be . . .*" I whisper.

We finish together. "*A poet.*"

"It's definitely Constance," Adam says.

"I feel bad now," I confess. "We shouldn't've written in it. I just . . . I just wanted it to be ours, and I didn't think . . . I mean, I hoped, but I didn't really believe . . . And now . . . It should be in a museum or a library. The diary of Constance Brooke. I can't even get my head around how I'll tell my mother that we—"

"We didn't damage it," Adam says firmly. "We just wrote our names. And one Shakespeare line. The diary part is fine. Plus, she can't blame us for thinking it was blank."

He frowns again.

The ink seems much darker now. I can't see how we missed it before.

"We're just getting used to it," I suggest

But the possibility of the book writing back surfaces again . . .

Mr. Cates appears behind us. "How's it going?"

"Great!" I gush, slapping my arm across the page. "We're writing about memory."

He nods as if to say, "Of course you are," and pounces on the next pair of desks.

"Do you think we should turn the book in?" Adam whispers. He looks the way he did when we were eight, terrified to confess that we'd erased Shelby's history project off the computer.

I bite the inside of my cheek. Yes, we should turn it in, but I say, "No," and I force myself to sound confident. "Like you said, maybe Constance left the diary for someone to use. Anyway, it's ours now, and possession is half the law."

"Nine-tenths."

"Whatever. No one's looking for this." I've convinced myself. "No one wants it."

Neither of us points out that just because no one knows the diary exists doesn't mean it isn't valuable. That the right thing would be to hand it over to my mom. Or to Mr. Cates, who has perched on his desk again and is reading a poem to himself. He's smiling.

I smile too. "He said to use whatever inspires us."

Adam looks from Mr. Cates to the diary to me. His face is set.

"Our secret?" I offer my pinky.

Adam wraps his pinky around mine, and we move our locked fingers from my forehead to his, adding this promise to a long line that stretches back beyond my memory.

I shift the bookmark out of the way, and the strong scent of rosemary brings with it flashes of the island, where that piney smell infuses everything. Long, desperate games of Capture the Flag. Shelby lifting me up so I could hide the flag in the crook of a tree. Adam throwing and throwing and throwing the boat rope until he could lasso like Indiana Jones. Shelby reading aloud from *The Golden Compass* and then all of us playing that we were hiding from the Gobblers, who snatch children and, worse, snatch their souls, even though Shelby was technically too old to play pretend by then.

"Listen to this." Adam pulls me back to now. *"The rosemary thrives."* His eyes are wide, and his voice is just louder than a sigh. "Do you think the book is really writing back?"

I want to say yes, but a more practical response comes out. "Constance and her dad lived on the island before the '24 flood. He's the one who planted the rosemary, remember?"

"Still, you, like, moved the bookmark, which is rosemary, and I mean, you actually *are* Rosemary, and then the book says—"

"The book doesn't 'say' anything. It was written a long time ago. Look." I use my most matter-of-fact voice. "It's weird the island has rosemary growing on it, as our science teachers always point out. But it's exactly because it's weird that it makes perfect sense she would mention it in her diary." I don't know why I'm working so hard to stifle the thrill that wants to rise up.

Adam gives me a long look. "Okay."

Mr. Cates sets down his book, holds out his arms like a preacher, and summons our attention. "Class, the bell will ring in two minutes. Next session we'll be in the library so you can start to research your poet's biography. You'll need to select your poet by then."

Adam and I look at each other, and we don't need to say anything. Of course our poet will be Constance Brooke.

Mr. Cates continues, "Get down your last thoughts before the bell chases away the muse."

I turn back to Adam. "We can't write—"

"We already did," Adam reminds me, turning ahead to the middle of the book. "This page is blank."

I peer at it closely to make sure. No faded writing appears.

I take a breath like I'm jumping into cold water and write, *Words outlast stone. Poems are words.*

"Very clever," Adam snorts.

"Fine. You do it."

Rosemary remembers, he scrawls. *Rosemary is an herb and a person.*

"You started off well," I say.

We watch the page, waiting to see if the book will write back. It doesn't, of course. How could it?

My brain is still untangling equations from algebra when Adam grabs my arm and steers me toward the library. "Let's look at the diary over lunch."

I fall into step beside him. "We can try to read more of what Constance wrote on that one page." What if she wrote on more pages?

We walk through the metal detector, and Adam calls out, "Hey, Mrs. W! It's cool if we eat in here, right?"

"Just clean up after yourselves." She smiles behind the big checkout counter.

"I thought you weren't supposed to eat in the library," I mutter, as we wend between tables over to a sunny corner in the biography section.

"Yeah. At some point, there was a big reversal on that. I guess they figure we can take the books home and slobber all over them."

I set the diary between us and open to the page with writing—Constance's, not ours.

Adam arranges the components of his lunch according to some system. He has one of those lunchboxes that's a set of small containers, and each compartment holds something different. Grapes. Baby carrots tucked in a tidy row. Finally a sandwich, which he extracts from its box.

He catches me studying him. "What?"

The way he sorts everything helps hold the huge, messy shapelessness of life together. But I don't say that because it would be weird. "You're weird," I say instead, but he knows I don't mean it.

He starts to summarize what happened with the diary. "You wrote the rosemary line from *Hamlet* . . ." he says.

I repeat the line: *Rosemary, that's for remembrance. Pray, love, remember.*

He continues. "And then we noticed Constance's writing."

"Which is really faint," I add.

"So we didn't see it before," he says. "Even though we looked pretty carefully."

"But we should have seen it." I say what we both know. "It isn't that faded."

"You think there's actually something strange happening with this book?" His voice is just louder than his breath.

"Don't you?"

He nods. Once.

We both lean over the book, careful to hold our food away, and read together: *Father says we . . .*

The next word is blotted, like it got wet. The letters are frayed around the edges, tiniest hairs of ink reaching out into the roughness of the page.

Need. Adam works it out.

Father says we need the rosemary so that we can remember.

"Remember what?" I wonder, as I turn the page.

My hand flies to my mouth. Adam and I recoil. The new page just says *Wilkie.* Over and over and over and over. The whole page. Filled with the name Wilkie, written neatly at first and then more and more messily. And then it's blotchy, like rain fell on the page, drops of water, staining the cursive with pale brown blots. *Wilkie. Wilkie. Wilkie. Wilkie.*

Adam whispers, "So that we can remember *Wilkie.*"

Four

We both leap up, and Adam yanks me away from the table. My wooden chair pitches backwards and clatters to the floor.

"Everything okay?" Mrs. Wallace calls.

"Yup!" I squeak. Adam gives an awkward thumbs-up. It's good that Mrs. Wallace isn't looking too closely, because all the color has drained from Adam's face except two weird red blotches low on his cheeks.

I take a steadying breath. "It's just a name. Written over and over."

"That's the creepy part." Adam hugs himself. "You can tell something was wrong."

"But whatever was wrong was a long time ago. It's not wrong anymore."

"You don't know that," Adam counters. "If Wilkie, like, died, then he's still dead."

"Yeah, and that's sad, but everyone from history is dead. The tragedy is over."

"So why are you standing over here and not sitting with the perfectly harmless, not-at-all-weird diary there on the table?" he challenges.

"You pulled me!"

He reaches for my hand. "Together?"

"Together."

Before we can sit back down, the bell rings, and we automatically start stowing our lunch stuff.

I stash the diary in my backpack, where the bright colors of my other books shout, "Everything is fine here. Nothing to see. Move along."

We merge into the traffic of bodies moving every which way in the hall. "Who do you think Wilkie was?" Adam asks, dodging a tiny sixth-grader with a supersized backpack.

"How would I know?" I wave at Aileen. "Someone gone, I guess, otherwise they wouldn't have to worry about remembering him." I want all those Wilkies burned in my brain to go away. "Let's just put it out of our heads."

We walk together into social studies and slide into our seats.

Adam's not putting it out of his head. I can tell because his tongue pokes out of the corner of his mouth, which means he's puzzling through something.

I speak fast and low. "Since the book is so old, Wilkie's obviously dead. There's really nothing we can—"

He cuts me off. "We can show Shelby."

It's like the ground was crooked and just righted itself. Shelby will know how to respond to *Wilkie, Wilkie, Wilkie.*

Adam looks at me closely. "You don't mind, do you?"

"No! Why would I? Besides, we already showed her."

"Yeah, but we thought it was blank. Plus, you didn't want to show your mom."

"That's different. She has her own thing with books, but Shelby's thing is the same as our thing."

I move through the rest of the school day, listening and discussing and smiling. But Wilkie won't leave me alone, and I can't wait for Shelby to explain him away.

Adam and I stand under the overhang at the front of the middle school, staring at his phone, waiting for Shelby to text back.

Nothing.

I try *Need your help. Pick us up?* She can't ignore that.

But she does.

I call her. It doesn't even ring before her recorded voice trills happily, "Hey, this is Michelle. I'm busy right now. Leave a message."

Finally, Adam calls his dad at work. He turns away

from me while he talks, but the slump of his shoulders means his dad is being short in that I-don't-have-time-for-you-now way.

"He thinks she has rehearsal for the musical," he reports. "She's probably not allowed to have her phone on."

"At least she's not ignoring us," I sigh.

We amble toward home in a comfortable silence. We don't talk about the diary. We don't talk about how Shelby is always so busy, and instead of always being three, we're usually just two now.

On my wall, on the hook where Dad's stupid Escher print used to be, is the picture of the three of us that Adam gave me when we were nine. He painted down one side of the frame, *For My Best Friend,* and across the bottom, he painted *From Adam the Great,* and Shelby added *And His Super Sister* in little letters underneath because she took the picture, or actually her auto-timer thing took it. It's a close-up of the three of our faces. Shelby and I are cheek to cheek, with my brown hair and her blond hair all tumbled together. Adam's chin rests on top of my head, and his head tilts toward his sister's. We'd just finished doing a pajama march from my house to theirs, and we were proud of how silly and brave we were. On the two sides of the frame without any writing Adam drew sprigs of rosemary. For me.

Adam's house comes first. We both check our phones again.

"We'll come over when she gets home," he says. "If it's not too late."

It will be too late. It's already too late. I can't even remember why I thought it was so important to talk to Shelby. The book is really old and used to belong to a really famous poet, but it's mostly blank and not actually all that interesting.

I head home alone, and for no reason at all, I think about when you pretend to throw a ball for a dog and it runs and searches and looks up, expectant and confused and just a little betrayed.

When I get home, Mom is waiting for me, all delighted with herself for having found bright yellow curtains with rainbow speckles.

"For your room!" she exclaims with a big smile. "Do you love them?"

I stand on the stepladder, and Mom hands me the metal bar with the curtain sleeved onto it. My arms aren't long enough to set both ends of the rod on the hooks, and one end falls out when I try to put the other one in place and then the other end falls out, and Mom and I start laughing. Finally, she takes my place on the ladder, and I step back to admire the splash of color at each window.

She wants a tour of where I've put everything, and I realize she has felt left out of the momentous business of moving me into a new room. It's hard to believe it's only been three days.

"I love how you organized the books."

Not for the first time, I consider how Mom and Adam are a lot alike.

"Adam and I were thinking maybe this used to be Constance's room. You know, when she lived here."

"Maybe." Mom smiles. "That's a nice thought."

We go down to the den, and each of us curls up on one end of the couch, with our toes just touching in the middle. She's reading some massive nineteenth-century novel with the spine all creased and lots of pencil marks all over the margin, which means she's rereading. So am I. I flip ahead to the scene in *Harry Potter and the Chamber of Secrets* where Harry starts writing in the old diary he found, and I disappear into the story.

At eight thirty, after I've gone up to my room, Shelby calls. She's so sorry she missed my call. The musical rehearsals are crazy long but so much fun. I should totally try out when I get to the high school next year. Everyone's so nice. Blah. Blah. Blah.

"Anyway, what's up?" she asks.

"What did Adam tell you?"

"He said it was about the diary, but he got weird and wouldn't say more."

"Yeah, we were using the diary for our poetry journal. For Mr. Cates? And this writing kind of appeared," I falter. I can't summon the image of the words on the page.

"Uh-huh." Shelby doesn't even try to keep the skepticism out of her voice.

"It did!" I exclaim. "It really did write back."

"Are you reading *Chamber of Secrets* again?"

"No," I lie.

"Okay. So, what did it say?" She doesn't believe me, but the faintest hope that I might be telling the truth lifts her voice.

Why can't I remember? "Hang on."

I pull the diary from my backpack. The sweet, musty scent of old book rises from the parchment as I turn page after page. *Diary of a Poet*. The list of herbs. The line from *Hamlet*. Our lame notes from class. And nothing more.

"I . . . it's nothing." It is nothing, but it wasn't. Was it?

"You okay, Rosie?" The skepticism is replaced with kindness and concern.

No, I'm not okay. I think I'm going crazy. But I don't say that. I make an excuse about being tired.

"Is Adam still up?" I ask.

"You know he keeps the schedule of a toddler," she quips.

"Why does he do that?"

"Always has," she replies. "You sure you're okay?"

I could tell her. I could tell her the book was blank and then it wasn't and now it is again, but is that really what happened? Maybe Adam and I just wanted so badly to find something in the diary that we imagined we did. But my chair clattering to the floor in the library echoes in my head. We did see something. I'm sure of it.

"The book . . ." I begin. "It's . . . strange."

"It's pretty different, that's for sure," Shelby says.

She's waiting for me to offer more of an explanation, but I don't know what to say. My throat tightens like I might cry.

"Yeah. Really different," I choke out. "I gotta go."

"Okay." She sounds uneasy. "But call me back if you want."

I nod but can't speak, so I just hang up. I use all my strength to hold tears at bay. I thrust the book back into the cupboard, where it had waited for who knows how long to come out and confuse me and torment me. I slam the door shut.

In the morning, I stand in the middle of my room, biting the inside of my cheek and trying to decide whether or not I should take the diary to school. When the honk summons me, I tear down the stairs to the front door, but then I pivot and dash back up. Yank open the cupboard and grab the book. The cracked leather cover feels like skin. I don't want to touch it. I shove the book into my backpack.

I pull the front door closed behind me and climb into the Steiners' back seat.

"Hi, Michelle." The name is awkward in my mouth. "I thought your mom was driving."

"She had to be at work early," Adam grumbles.

"This is great, actually." I unzip my backpack. "I can show you what we found in the diary."

"What did we find?" Adam twists to look at me over his shoulder.

My memory of the afternoon in the library has gone fuzzy around the edges. Why can't I remember what we thought was so strange? "Was it writing?"

I open the book to the notes Adam made in class. *Rosemary remembers. Rosemary is an herb* . . . And back again to my handwriting, the line from *Hamlet* perched neatly at the top of a page, a page that is otherwise blank.

I look up at Adam. His mouth is open slightly, as if he's forgotten what he was going to say. He faces front and runs a hand through his hair.

"I can't look while I'm driving, Rosie," Shelby says. She steers around the curve on River Road, her eyes straight ahead, her hands perfectly positioned on the wheel.

I keep a hand on the book, waiting for a chance. Maybe at a traffic light. I look past Shelby to the island. The bare trees of winter make it look forlorn and incomplete.

Last time the three of us went there, we paddled through the leaves drifting on the water. Shelby and I worked the oars while Adam lounged in the front of the boat and sang loudly and badly in made-up Italian.

We tied up the boat and carried our picnic to the rosemary patch, which Shelby calls the Rosie patch. While we ate, we plotted a play version of some book we were reading. I don't remember what it was. We were always planning plays and casting them and collecting costumes and props and then the actual play would only take about three minutes, and the Steiners wouldn't be able to make it, and Mom would gush about how we'd done such a great job, and we'd start in on the next one.

"Do you guys have Mr. Cates today?" Shelby asks.

"Yeah. We're meeting in the library."

"For biography research," Adam adds.

Shelby sighs. "I loved that class. It was way better than ninth-grade English. Who're you doing for your project?"

"Constance Brooke," I answer.

"Really?" Shelby glances at me in the rearview mirror.

"Yeah, because of the diary," I explain.

She swoops into the drive in front of the school. Adam's already climbing out of the car.

"I really want to show you—" I start, but the person behind us honks.

"Sorry." She tucks her hair behind her ears. "Later, okay?"

We stand together and watch Shelby pull away.

Mr. Cates is waiting with Mrs. Wallace in the reference section. The rest of our class is already scattered around a handful of square tables for four.

"Welcome!" Mr. Cates beams at us. He explains how we'll research the poets we've chosen and then tomorrow, we'll start assembling our poetry projects. Working with our partners, we'll put together a binder of poems by our poet but also poems we write that are inspired by the poet. "A conversation in verse," Mr. Cates explains.

Mrs. Wallace leads us to a bank of computers and shows us how to find this online thing called the *Dictionary of Literary Biography.* She demonstrates how it works by looking up Shakespeare. I study the portrait of him while she talks about the different kinds of information we can find.

"He had earrings!" I whisper to Adam.

He grins. "Like a pirate."

"Thank you, Mrs. Wallace," Mr. Cates says. "All right, folks, we only have about forty minutes before the bell, so get to work." He hands out half sheets of blue paper with the assignment printed in a medieval-looking font.

Adam reads the instructions while I pull the diary from my bag. "For the biography part, we're supposed to learn about our poet's life and pick some detail that interests us. Then we're supposed to read poems by the poet that might be about that detail and also write our own poems about it. Like, if we pick the fact that our poet had a dog, we could write about our own dog." He looks up at me. "Except neither of us has a dog, so a different detail than that. Obviously."

"Mr. Cates?" I raise my hand. "Adam and I want to do Constance Brooke. Is that okay?"

"I thought you jaded citizens of Cookfield felt overexposed to the celebrated Constance Brooke," he replies.

"Yeah." Adam shrugs. "But since Rosemary lives in her house and all, we thought, you know, it could be, uh, interesting."

"Indeed!" Mr. Cates smiles and pushes his curls back. "You may certainly research whatever poet you find 'uh, interesting.'"

He winks at us and goes to help Josh and Alex, who are pretending they don't know how to get off YouTube.

I set the diary next to the keyboard, where its ancient, cracked cover looks just plain wrong.

Adam clicks through to the biography site and types *Constance Brooke* in the search box. The first thing that comes up is an entry from *Twentieth-Century American Poets.*

"Wow!" I say as Adam scrolls down the list of publications. "She wrote a lot more than twenty poems!"

He gets to the actual biography part, and we read together. She was born in Cookfield in 1914. Her father, Arthur, taught Shakespeare at the university.

"Like your mom," Adam points out.

Constance lived with her parents on an island in the river. We already know this. I start skimming. Her mother died in the 1919 flu pandemic when Constance was five.

"That's sad!" I exclaim.

"What?" Adam catches up. "Oh, that sucks. So it was just her and her dad, I guess."

Now we're both skimming. The 1924 flood destroyed their house. They moved into town. Into my house. Early writing, which they call juvenilia.

Maybe I should write *juvenilia* in the diary—it is our poetry journal after all—but I don't want to open the book. I try to pin down whatever is making me uneasy, but it skitters away.

"Maybe we shouldn't . . ." I begin.

Adam glances at me. "It's too late to worry about writing in it, Rosie. Just go ahead."

"Okay," I agree, but my stomach churns, like when I have to do a presentation in front of the whole class. I find the page where we jotted notes yesterday and write *juvenilia* at the top and then = *writing she did when she was a kid.*

"Does that mean our poems are juvenilia?"

Adam cocks his head. "I think it's only juvenilia if you become a famous writer. It's, like, retroactive."

Mr. Cates appears out of nowhere and squats next to us. "Have you selected your detail?"

"Not yet," Adam replies, his eyes still on the screen, his finger on the scroll button.

Mr. Cates looks at me. "Perhaps the house? An obvious choice, I'd think."

"Maybe," I say. "Maybe both houses. You know, the ruin on the island and my house. Her house, I mean. But also memory . . ." I try to put together a thought about the stones of the ruined house and monuments and memory.

"Look up her poem 'Moon Mangled Memory.' It may speak to you. Let the muse do her work . . ." His voice goes slightly spooky, and he wanders off to Kendall and Aileen, who wouldn't know the muse if she smacked them in the face.

"Is the muse speaking to you?" I whisper.

Adam looks me in the eye and raises one eyebrow. I love that he can do that and hate that I can't.

He opens a new window and searches for "Moon Mangled Memory." It comes right up. I lean in so we can both read it off the screen. It begins *We mark time by the moon.*

I read the first line of the second stanza aloud. *Math of shadow and light.* "That's cool."

Adam picks up farther down:

> A new moon is nothing.
> A beginning that is
> Absence, blankness and void.

"Kind of creepy," he says.

I read the last stanza:

> A new moon is nothing.
> No light. No sight. Recall
> Only darkness. Absent
> Souvenir. All is lost.

I'm puzzled. "I don't really get how it's about memory."

"Yeah," Adam says. "It's more about the moon."

"And maybe forgetting." The vagueness of the poem clarifies just a little. "There's all that 'nothing' and 'darkness' stuff. And the title says *mangled* memory, like memory is damaged, which would be the same as forgetting, I guess."

"Is it speaking to you?" Adam asks.

"Not yet. I need more time."

"I don't have thyme, but I have rosemary," Adam jokes, waving the rosemary bookmark in my face.

"What a dork," Kendall says behind me. "Why are you friends with him?"

The pine smell rises off the bookmark and summons images of books and boats and costumes. I'm friends with him because I always have been, and not even the boys-are-gross years separated us. I wouldn't be me without Adam.

"Shut up, Kendall," I snap.

Adam gives me a look layered with gratitude and worry.

I take the bookmark and match his bad pun with my own. "You are so sage. Get it? Like, wise?"

"I get it, Rosie. At least, parsley." He laughs a sharp bark of a laugh. "Like partly?"

"Parsley, sage, rosemary, and thyme," I murmur.

"We should write that down!"

"Why?" I ask, but I turn to the next page.

The heavy parchment almost resists.

And there it is. The thing I couldn't grab before. *Remember Wilkie. Wilkie. Wilkie.*

"Wilkie." I whisper the name, half expecting that the words on the page will disappear.

Adam swallows. Turns back to the screen and pages down, seeking an explanation. "There's no Wilkie in the biography."

"He had to be important," I say. "For her to write his name over and over like that."

"We could ask her!" He perks up. "We should go see her."

"Go see her?" This had never crossed my mind.

"At River House," Adam explains. "She still lives there, right? So, let's go ask her about Wilkie."

"But we don't know her," I protest. The theory of Constance is one thing. The reality is something else altogether.

"She's an old lady in a nursing home." Adam dismisses my anxiety. "She'll be happy to have visitors."

When our second-grade class sang holiday songs at River House, the people didn't seem happy about much of anything. A group of hunched white-haired people smiled vaguely or slept or stared at something the rest of us couldn't see.

"Maybe she just wants to be left alone," I worry.

"It can't hurt to try."

"I don't know," I say. "It seems like an invasion of her privacy."

"We already crossed that line when we read her diary," Adam replies.

"I . . . okay," I concede. "I guess we could go."

Adam checks the clock. "We have a few minutes. Let's get our thoughts organized. You know, sort out what we understand about the book and figure out what we want to ask her."

Out of nowhere, Adam produces graph paper and is happily drawing boxes. He writes *Constance* in one and *Herb Person* in another.

"You should add our writing," I suggest. I point to the *Hamlet* quote. "It didn't vanish."

Adam adds *A&R* in a third box.

"Maybe Shelby could come with us," I say.

"She'll have rehearsal again. Anyway, we don't need her." He says it too loud, and Mr. Cates starts to make his way toward us.

We pretend to be busy with our research.

I copy a good line from the biography: *The flood was stronger than stone.*

"That's when it became a ruin," Adam observes.

"Imagine!" Mr. Cates leans in. Maybe he thinks he's our muse. "Imagine your home as a ruin."

I dutifully picture my room with the new curtains

in tatters and the walls broken and jagged, the roof torn away so daylight slants on the muddied floor. My books swollen and coated in slime, the cupboard door gaping open like a wound.

"Rosie"—Adam checks to make sure Mr. Cates is out of earshot—"do you think the book . . ." He swallows and puts more confidence in his voice. "Do you think it could actually be magical?"

My heart yearns toward yes. Books I love say yes, but the fluorescent lights and the computer screen and the partners chattering around us all say no.

"I wish it could be," I say. "I mean, part of me hopes . . . but it just seems so unlikely."

Adam looks away.

Suddenly, I remember two years ago, when Adam and I wanted to do a talent show. Shelby refused. She said she was too old. Adam said just he and I could do it. He stood there with a handful of piano music and some silly hats, two on his head at once. But I followed Shelby's lead, and I laughed at him. He looked so wounded. I felt awful.

And now I've disappointed him again.

"I'm sorry." I have tears in my eyes now. "I'm just trying to understand. And it doesn't make sense, and that . . . that freaks me out."

He stares at the boxes he made.

I try to meet him on the stable ground of graph paper and organizing things. "Here are possibilities. One: We're crazy . . ."

Adam sits up and labels a new list *Theories* and writes *1. Crazy.*

"Two: We're having a collective hallucination."

He looks confused.

"Like at the Salem witch trials," I explain.

He adds *2. Hallucination.*

"Three . . ." I take a breath and set skepticism aside. "It's magic." And possibilities from books crowd together in my head and scramble over each other with glee. Portals and ghosts and time travel.

Adam grins and writes in all capital letters: *3. MAGIC.*

Five

MOM DIDN'T WANT to take us to River House, but now we're sitting in the car, which idles in the U-shaped drive in front of the nursing home. Mom's twisted around so she can look at us in the back seat. She speaks slowly, choosing her words: "Constance Brooke is a great poet, and she was a kind woman—I met her when we bought the house. But she is old—very old, nearly a hundred—and she has Alzheimer's. Her memory is terrible, and she's not who she used to be. It's great that you're taking your poetry project so seriously, but you may not find her very helpful."

"It's okay, Mom," I assure her, but I'm not anxious to go inside.

"We understand," Adam agrees earnestly.

"I'll be back right here to pick you up in an hour," she says, then hesitates. "Are you sure you don't want me to . . . ? We could all go in together . . ."

"No," I say sharply.

"We'll be fine," Adam says. "Really."

"Okay," she sighs.

We dart out of the car before she can change her mind and hurry through the automatic glass doors into a sterile lobby.

"Can I help you?" A woman sits at a reception desk peeking through an aggressive arrangement of fake flowers.

"We're looking for Constance Brooke," I say.

I space out while she gives directions, but Adam listens, and he leads the way down a long corridor. I puzzle over the strange smell. Overcooked broccoli and cleaning liquid and something else.

I tug the rosemary bookmark out of my bag and clutch it close to my face, letting its piney scent overpower the sad odor of the nursing home.

Doubts swirl around me like dry leaves. "This isn't a good idea. This place is . . . is sad, and the smell . . ."

Adam grips my arm and pulls me along with him. "It is a good idea, Rosemary. She can tell us about the flood and also about . . ." He searches for the name.

"Wilkie," I say. "But what if she doesn't remember him?"

"She can't have forgotten someone whose name she wrote over and over like that. Even with Alzheimer's, she'll be able to tell us who Wilkie is."

He leads us into a sunroom, decorated with white

wicker furniture and gentle floral prints. The room tries too hard to be pleasant.

A man wearing skin two sizes too big sits in a wheelchair, his hands crumpled like talons awkwardly in his lap, his mouth open. Spit drools down his chin and onto a terry cloth bib tied around his neck. His eyes are open, but he doesn't seem to see anything. He moans, low and rhythmically. Then, offbeat, with a gruesome syncopation, he shouts, "You're not Maud!"

We hurry past him toward a table where two women sit across from each other. Each holds a handful of cards. This seems more promising.

"I said hearts, Anna!" cries the nearest woman. Her gray hair is messily pulled back into a Hello Kitty clip.

"No, clubs," the other answers, shaking her white head dramatically.

A mess of cards lies scattered under the table. They can't really be playing a game when they're missing so many cards. Adam kneels down and starts to gather them up.

"We're looking . . ." My voice comes out in a whisper. I clear my throat and start again. "We're looking for Constance Brooke."

Anna stares at me, her jaw clenching and unclenching like a ventriloquist's dummy. Suddenly, she barks, "I'll take the pot pie."

I don't know what to do. Adam stands and puts

the cards in a neat stack on the table. He asks, "Do you know where Constance Brooke is?"

The Hello Kitty woman stares at Adam. Anna stares at me. Suddenly, as if on cue, they both turn back to their cards.

"I said hearts, Anna!"

"No, clubs!"

It's like *Alice in Wonderland* here, only the people in Wonderland make more sense. I pluck at Adam's sleeve and edge toward the door.

A soft voice rises from the corner. "Constance is in her room. Down the hall. That way." A bony finger points to the left. The finger is attached to a tiny woman in a bright red dress.

"Thank you." I smile at her, grateful that someone seems to be sane.

She smiles back, and her smile is too large for her face, like the Cheshire Cat's smile. It really is Wonderland in here.

We escape into the corridor. The wheelchair man's low moans follow us, and I jump when he shouts, "You're not Maud!"

"No one should have to live like this," Adam whispers.

"Can I help you?" A nurse stops us near a bend in the corridor. She holds a small cup of pills in one hand and a battered clipboard in the other.

"We're looking for Constance Brooke."

I try to muffle the desperation in my voice, but I'm sure she notices. Maybe everyone who comes here is a little desperate.

"You're not family." She studies us over the clipboard.

Adam babbles an explanation about our poetry project.

"Room fifty-five. Just ahead on the left." She walks past us, but the professional clack of her heels halts. She lowers the clipboard. "You know Miss Brooke suffers from Alzheimer's disease? At her stage, she has lost most of her adult life."

"What does that mean?" Adam asks.

"Her memory has diminished significantly. Most of the time she's in the 1920s."

I do some quick math. "So she thinks she's a child?"

"Not exactly, but she doesn't remember being an adult." She notices the pills in her hand, and with a tight, frazzled smile, she clacks away.

"I think forgetting your own life might be the saddest thing I've ever heard of," I say.

Adam sighs. "She won't remember Wilkie."

"Maybe we shouldn't . . ."

"Maud!"

The sharp voice from the sunroom drives me forward with the vague sense that we owe Constance

Brooke the gift of our right minds. Maybe we won't learn anything from her, but at least we can talk to her and be people in her present who aren't demented.

The door to room fifty-five is ajar, and I tap lightly.

"Yes?"

We walk together into the small room.

Constance Brooke is so frail it hardly seems possible that she's alive. Her silver white hair almost gives off light, like LED Christmas lights. It's held away from her face by a black velvety headband and curls in wisps to her jaw, which sticks out as if daring her faded skin to wither away. She's neatly dressed in a white blouse with a bow at the neck and a sky blue skirt that flares just past her knees.

"Come in," she says, her pale cheeks widening into a gentle smile. "Do I know you?"

"No," I answer. I don't know what to say.

Adam clears his throat. "I'm Adam. Adam Steiner. This is Rosemary Bennett. We're, uh, doing a project—"

"I live in your house," I blurt out. This seems more to the point than our stupid poetry assignment.

Constance frowns, her eyes dimming a little. The headband tips slightly as her brow wrinkles in confusion. "My house?" Her voice is wispy like her hair, as if she doesn't have enough breath for speech. "But my house is gone. Destroyed in the flood. At the new moon."

"No, I don't live on the island," I explain. "I live in the house you moved to after the flood. On Pear Tree Lane."

"Pear Lane?" She frowns.

"Pear Tree Lane."

She closes her eyes, as if looking for the house in her mind. When she opens them, her face is blank. She notices us. Her paper cheeks arc into soft folds as she smiles. "Hello. Do I know you?"

No. You don't know us. You don't even know yourself.

Adam speaks slowly, carefully. "I'm Adam. This is Rosemary. We were asking about your house. Your house on Pear Tree Lane."

She shakes her head. "I'm sorry. You must have the wrong person. I lived on the island. A lovely stone house. Gone now."

"She doesn't remember," I murmur.

"Miss Brooke," Adam presses. "Could you tell us about Wilkie?"

"Wilkie? I'm afraid I don't . . ." She plucks at her skirt. Her gaze wanders out of focus.

"Miss Brooke?"

Her attention settles on us again. "Hello! I'm so

sorry. I've forgotten my manners. Do I know you? I'm Constance."

Adam swallows and repeats, "I'm Adam Steiner. This is Rosemary Bennett."

"Rosemary?" Constance's eyes settle on me, but her focus turns inward. "Father is magical with rosemary. Can get it to grow anywhere. He says he could make a rosemary farm at the North Pole, and I don't doubt it. Simply magical." She adjusts her headband. Seems to see us for the first time. "How do you do? I am Constance Brooke."

"I'm Adam." He tries to sound cheerful. "This is Rosemary."

"Rosemary? Father is magical with rosemary. He says—"

"I live in your house." I cut in. "The house on Pear Tree Lane. The one you lived in after the flood."

"After the flood?" She shudders. Closes her eyes.

"Let's go," I mouth. This is too awful.

Adam holds up one finger.

Constance opens her eyes. "Hello," she says with a slight smile. "Would you like some candy?" She reaches an impossibly thin arm out toward a nightstand, where a porcelain dish holds a few battered peppermints.

"No, thank you." I swallow the urge to cry.

Adam looks at me, his eyebrows arched. What now?

Maybe the diary is still there, clinging to her memory. When I'm old, I'm sure I won't forget the books I've loved. I couldn't.

"Do you remember hiding a book in a cupboard? A very old book?" I ask.

She folds her hands in her lap. "An old book? Perhaps you mean Father's false codex?"

"I—I don't know." I look at Adam.

"What's a false codex?" Adam asks.

"He's magical with rosemary, you know," she sighs. "Less magical with Shakespeare." She makes a breathy sound that might be a laugh but quickly becomes a cough.

"Is the false codex about Shakespeare?" In my head, Mr. Cates reminds me that we breathe Shakespeare like oxygen.

"Father believes . . ." Her voice trails off.

"What did your father believe?"

"Nothing to do with me," she says. "Would you like some candy?" She gestures again toward the sad peppermints.

Adam nudges me. "Show her the book."

"But it might . . ." I was going to say *hurt her,* but how could it? I pull the diary from my bag. "Do you remember this?"

She takes it from me, and her arms collapse onto her lap with the weight of it.

She rests a translucent hand on the burgundy cover. "It took him away," she whispers. She looks from me to Adam, her eyes wide.

"Who?" I ask.

"Father is always working," she whimpers.

"Mine too," Adam says in a low voice.

She opens the cover and strokes the list of names. "I wrote my name. I knew I shouldn't . . . I was angry." She frowns. "But these others . . . do I know them? Rosemary Bennett. Adam Steiner." She pronounces our names phonetically as if reading a foreign language. "Do I know them?" She looks up at us with wide eyes and an aimless smile.

"I'm Rosemary," I answer. "He's Adam."

"It's so very nice to meet you," she recites.

"You were telling us about the false codex," Adam prompts.

"Was I?" Her tone is bland.

"And something about Shakespeare," I add.

"Yes." She nods. "It's always about Shakespeare."

"We wondered if you know . . ." The name escapes me. Who did we want to ask her about?

Constance turns pages. *The Diary of a Poet*. The list of herbs. Blank and blank and more blank. She keeps turning.

Adam says, "It seemed like there wasn't any more

writing in the book, and then there was . . ." He trails off, confused.

The image of blotchy cursive haunts me, but what did it say? "Writing appeared," I affirm. "And then it was gone."

Constance nods sympathetically as she turns page after page. "Yes, it happens like that."

"*What* happens?" Adam and I ask together.

She keeps turning pages. "Nothing and more nothing, and then words come and you remember . . ."

"What?" Adam asks. "What do you remember?"

"Nothing," she says in a monotone. "It disappears."

"Is she describing the diary or her mind?" I whisper.

A yellowed page rests against Constance's palm. "So old," she murmurs. "You can feel that this page was once something living. It has life in it still, but also decay."

"You remember the book," Adam observes.

"The false codex," she murmurs. "How could I forget?"

"What's a false codex?" I ask.

"A foolishness more than a lie," she sighs. "If there is a bear in Shakespeare and here is a bear, would you conclude that it must be Shakespeare's bear? Of course not. Foolishness."

"Bear?" I frown at Adam. "Where is there a bear?"

She tips her head up and searches my face. In the searching, she seems to lose her way, and her eyes drift to the dish at her side. "Would you care for some candy?" Her arm extends toward the dish.

"No, thank you."

"Rosie, look." Adam points to the open book. My notes, unchanged, easy to read, sit at the top of the page. *Juvenilia. Mom died in flu pandemic.*

"It doesn't make any sense," I exclaim. "What I wrote is here, but the other writing . . ."

Constance presses her skeletal hands against her eyes and breathes out, a long slow exhale. "Void and nothing," she says through her breath.

"What is that?" I ask. "What does that mean?"

She doesn't respond. She starts turning pages again. Slow. Steady. The only sound in the bright room is the gentle movement of parchment, a dry sound, like dead leaves.

"My hands remembered the way," Constance says, quietly triumphant. Her bony fingers scrabble against the page.

"It's folded in!" I cry out.

Adam and I huddle over the book. I reach into the crease of the binding and fumble for an edge. Find it. I peel the page open. Like one of those foldouts in a little-kid book that opens up to show a bigger picture or a map, only there's no picture here.

There are words. Six lines of faded handwriting. A poem.

"I'm sorry," Constance whispers.

"No!" Adam grins. "This is amazing! Thank you!"

The poem is in the same old-fashioned writing as the list of herbs. It will take some work to figure out what it says.

"Did you write this?" I ask.

Constance shakes her head. Her green eyes swim with tears. "I'm sorry. I knew better."

"It's okay," I reassure her, though I'm not sure what she means.

"My hands remembered the way," she says again, and she turns her hands over and stares at them with wonder.

Six

IN THE CAR, Mom pumps us for information about the visit.

"You were right," I tell her. "Her memory is really bad. She was nice to us . . ."

"Kept offering us candy," Adam interjects.

"But she didn't make any sense. She said this really weird thing about a bear in Shakespeare—"

"Did she?" Mom perks up. "That actually does make sense. There is a bear in Shakespeare."

"There is?" Adam and I exclaim in unison.

"Yes, it's in *The Winter's Tale.* You know there aren't a lot of stage directions in Shakespeare's plays?"

"No, but okay." She always imagines I have the same random information taking up space in my head that she has in hers.

"Well, I think it's in Act Three. One of Shakespeare's rare stage directions is *exeunt, pursued by a bear.*" She smiles. "So perhaps Constance Brooke was making more sense than you realized."

"What's *exeunt*?" Adam asks.

"Exit in the plural," Mom says.

"So people were being chased by a bear?" I ask.

"Yup!" Our actually wanting to talk about Shakespeare has delighted her into forgetting about the depressing report of our visit to River House.

"Do you think she was trying to tell us about a bear?" Adam puzzles.

"No." I watch the ruin of Constance's old house whiz by as we drive down River Road. "It was more like a metaphor."

"For what?"

"No clue," I sigh.

"Does *false codex* mean anything to you, Claudia?" Adam asks.

Mom's eyes snap to meet mine in the rearview mirror. "She didn't really mention the false codex, did she?"

"Yeah, what is it?"

She does that sniff laugh she uses when something's not really funny. "It's the reason we came to Cookfield."

"Sorry?" This is the last thing I expected her to say. "I thought we came because you got a job at the university."

"We did, but I wanted the job because Arthur Brooke, who taught English here and who was Constance's father, did a lot of research on a book—a codex—that he believed belonged to Shakespeare. Most scholars think he was wrong—that's why they call it false—but I was enchanted by the idea that there might be something to discover about Shakespeare in Cookfield, so here we are."

"Did you get to study the codex?" I clutch at my bag.

"No," she answers. "Brooke left all sorts of interesting notes in the university archive, but the book was lost long before I showed up. It was a disappointment, but of course, it can't really have belonged to Shakespeare, so it's no great loss."

Adam and I sit on my bed, a pizza box between us.

"I kind of feel like we stole the book from your mom," Adam says through a mouthful of cheese he's pulled off the pizza. He always does this. He eats one piece. For the second piece, he pulls off the cheese and toppings and eats them as a gooey handful. Then last he'll just pick at the toppings. It would drive me crazy if he hadn't been doing this since we were two.

"She never knew it was in the house." Guilt swells up, and I set down my half-eaten slice. "I felt like we could take it, you know, because it was in my room, and no one wanted it. It had been left behind, forgotten. But . . . my own mother was looking for it!" I drop my head onto my knees. I can't tell her we found the diary—the codex—and wrote in it. But not telling her has suddenly become an enormous lie. I want to go back and find the book again and make a different choice.

"But, Rosie." Adam reaches for some way to make this better. "It can't really be Shakespeare's book. I mean, what are the chances? How could it be?" He picks pepperoni off the pizza.

"But what if it is?" I moan.

"Okay," he says in a firm voice. "Even if it is Shakespeare, all it has is a list of herbs and a short poem, so it's not like it's . . . important." He trails off as we both hear how lame this sounds.

"Maybe the disappearing writing was Shakespeare too, and we made it disappear!" Panic swirls around me. "Adam, we didn't just write in Shakespeare's diary. We somehow erased it!"

He wipes his hands. "Let's figure out the poem. Then we can decide what to do."

I push the pizza box to the floor and set the diary in its place. Unfold the page Constance's hands remembered. There are the six lines of old-fashioned writing.

"I can't read it at all." I squint at the loops and curls, faded to a thin gray shadow.

"Me either. Is it the same handwriting as the list of herbs?" Adam asks.

With the page unfolded, we can look at the poem and the list side by side. "Does the poem have those *f/s* things? I mean the *s*'s that look like *f*'s."

"Yes!" Adam exclaims. "Look at the second line. There are a bunch of those *f*'s. *S*'s. Whatever."

"And look at the third line. That's a capital *S*, I'm pretty sure, and it has that same loopiness as those ones. Look at *Sage.*"

Adam pulls his graph paper from his pocket. "The person who wrote the list also wrote the poem."

"And that person might be Shakespeare," I whimper.

"Might be." He stresses *might*, but he writes *Shakespeare* on his grid.

I reach across him and add a question mark: *Shakespeare?*

"And Constance also wrote in the book, but she didn't write the poem," I say. "So it might have said *Diary of a Poet* before it was hers."

"Or before she was even a poet," Adam adds.

We shift around so that we're lying on our stomachs with the book in front of us.

It takes almost an hour to figure out just the first two lines of the poem, and then Adam has to go because it's late and we have school tomorrow.

We stand in the foyer, and I hold the graph paper while he bundles into his coat. I read what we've figured out so far, printed neatly on the right side of the paper, each letter poised precisely on the line.

> Ah, treble words of absence spoken low;
> For ears of fam'ly, friend, or willful foe.

Fam'ly took us forever, and we had to look up *treble,* which means anything multiplied three times. Adam thought it had to do with music, which it does, but that's a different meaning. Or maybe both meanings matter. If we've learned nothing else from Mr. Cates, it's that words in poems often mean a bunch of things all at one time.

With his coat zipped up and his hat pulled down over his forehead, Adam looks like a little kid. "Rosie, could you wait till tomorrow to figure out the rest of the poem?"

"Of course!" I promise, in a gush of warmth for the little-kid Adam who's part of thirteen-year-old Adam. Both of them, all the Adams I remember, are my best friends. "Maybe Shelby will be able to come too," I suggest.

"I'll ask her," he promises as he heads out into the night.

Shelby doesn't have rehearsal, and she doesn't have plans with her friends, but we don't get to work on the poem. Mom needs some super-special old book from the big used bookstore in Lionville, and Shelby and Adam and I always love going there, so we're off on an unexpected excursion. In the car, we sing along to *Matilda* like we always used to, and I don't mind that the poem has to wait. Mom and Shelby try to outsoprano each other, while Adam experiments with his new baritone, and I hang out happily in the middle.

Eliot Books is the best kind of used bookstore. They always have what I'm looking for, as well as books I didn't even know to look for but that seem to have been looking for me. The irregular piles of books leaning in unsteady towers all over the place promise surprises. One time Shelby found an old novel called *To the Island*, and it seemed like it had been written just for us.

Mom heads to the back office to pick up the book she's come to get, and Adam and Shelby and I stand just inside the front door, breathing in the musty, sweet smell of the old books. The same smell as the diary.

The tall shelves form nooks. In some, the owners have put random chairs, here a hard-backed old-fashioned desk chair, there a small overstuffed armchair. The three of us like to crowd into the chair-and-a-half that fills the middle-grade-young-adult nook, and we wend our way past fiction and biography to get there. At English history, I realize we lost Shelby in fiction.

I turn back. "You coming?"

She doesn't look up from the book she's pulled from a pile propped against the *E*'s and *F*'s. Her long hair looks almost golden compared to all the browns and burgundies and greens of the old books that frame her. I have my phone. I could take a great photo of her. But I don't want a picture of Shelby in adult fiction.

"I thought maybe I'd tackle *The Mill on the Floss,*" she murmurs.

Our teachers are always mentioning *The Mill on the Floss.* It's about a small town on a river that floods, like ours. But they say we should read it when we're older. When we're adults. Once you cross over to *The Mill on the Floss,* you don't belong in the middle-grade nook anymore.

"Not yet, Shelby," I plead.

"Michelle," she corrects me absently, but she puts the book back on the stack and follows me to our spot.

Adam's already claimed the cushiest corner of the chair, and he holds a tan hardcover book with a title in gilt letters.

I squeeze next to him, and Shelby perches on the arm of the chair.

"What'd you find?" she asks.

"*The Story of the Amulet,* by E. Nesbit," he replies.

"I've never heard of that one." I read over his shoulder. *There were once four children who spent their summer holidays—*

"Why is it always summer holidays?" Shelby wonders. "Can't people have adventures in winter?"

"We're having an adventure in winter," I counter. "You know, the diary."

"Did you bring it?" She lowers her voice.

"No. I didn't want my mom to see it." Guilt pokes at me again.

Adam explains as best he can what Constance said, and he tells Shelby about the poem. I tune them out and sit, miserable with self-reproach.

Mom brought me to this bookstore. She brought me to books, period. She's the reason I even care about the diary, or the false codex, or whatever it is. All the books in the nook seem to be scolding me, and I shove myself out of the chair and move away.

"Rosie?" Adam calls after me.

"I want to see if they have anything by Constance." I made this up on the spot, but it's actually a good idea, and I pick my way around piles of books to the poetry section.

I step back to look up at the second-to-the-top shelf, well above my head. Brontë. Brooke. There are two books with Constance's name on the spine.

"What are you looking for?" Mom appears at my side, clutching a brown-wrapped package to her chest.

"Constance Brooke. For our poetry project," I answer. Gratitude and shame jostle each other. Gratitude that she didn't show up when we were talking about the diary. Shame that I'm grateful. "Did you get what you needed?"

She pats the package. "It's a rare eighteenth-century edition of Shakespeare's sonnets with some slight alterations. Most scholars have dismissed its authenticity, but I want to decide for myself." She's all lit up.

"I hope when I grow up I love my job as much as you do," I say.

She puts a hand on my cheek. "I hope so too, Rosie." She nods to the ladder. "See what you can find."

I climb up two steps. A little stack of paperback books sits on the platform at the top of the ladder. Constance's name leaps out at me from one of the paperbacks. *Constance Brooke—Early Poems.* I extract the slim book from the stack.

A black-and-white photo of a young Constance looks out solemnly from the cover. She must be in her twenties or so. Her hair is light and curly—wispy, even, as it is now—and she wears a headband. It's uncanny how much she looks like her aged self; wrinkles already line her forehead. She's framed by rows and rows of books, just as Shelby would have been if I'd taken her picture earlier.

I lean against the ladder, my elbows alongside the stack of paperbacks, and turn to the table of contents. "Moon Mangled Memory" is there.

"Can I get this?" I hold it up for Mom to see.

She smiles. "Sure!"

In the car, Shelby and Mom chatter about the musical. I didn't know that Shelby has a good part. She even has a solo. Mom was in the same show once upon a time, and they're deep in the details of the staging.

Adam and I flip through the book of poems. The pages are cool, with the slightest hint of damp.

A lot are about nature. Many are too abstract to make much sense to me.

When we get to "Moon Mangled Memory," I read it aloud.

"I still don't get how it's about memory," Adam says.

"Souvenir," Mom tosses over her shoulder. "*Souvenir* means memory."

Adam reads the last stanza again:

> A new moon is nothing.
> No light. No sight. Recall
> Only darkness. Absent
> Souvenir. All is lost.

"So, like, absent memory," he paraphrases.

"You were right," I point out. "It is about forgetting."

The poem on the facing page is called "Sifting Words." I'm starting to feel carsick and need to look away from the book. "Read that one," I suggest, and close my eyes.

> I sift words like sand. They run through my mind.

"Lovely image!" Mom exclaims.

> Ink strokes form letters bundled into words.
> Words join up with armies of phrases, lines,
> That march on iambic feet, singing rhyme.
> They enjamb boldly . . .

"What's enjamb?" Adam asks.

"When the sentence doesn't stop at the end of a line," I say. "Right?"

"Very good." Mom must think she's died and gone to heaven.

Adam continues reading:

> They enjamb boldly, aspire to meaning.
> They make speech and song and soliloquy.
> Gather into scenes and acts, renowned plays
> Famous from their day, unforgotten still.

"Is it about Shakespeare?" Shelby asks.

"Maybe," Mom says. "Sounds like it. And she was certainly familiar with Shakespeare through her father."

We're almost to Adam's house, so he just paraphrases the rest. "It says that plays and speeches and stuff aren't important. Only words matter. And then it's like she's looking for a certain word but can't find it." He reads:

> I rue the day I learned to seek, knowing
> I could never catch a word so well hid.

Mom pulls up in front of Adam and Shelby's house. They say thanks as they climb out of the car.

"We'll do the thing tomorrow," I call after them, and at least Adam knows what I mean.

Mom and I make dinner together and read a little on the couch before bed. I nudge her toes with mine. She looks up, in that daze of being lost in a book.

"We're sifting words." I echo Constance.

Delight breaks her daze. "Together."

Finally, Adam and I again lie on our stomachs with the book open in front of us, and Adam's graph paper tucked under his hand. I reread the first two lines:

Ah, treble words of absence spoken low;
For ears of fam'ly, friend, or willful foe.

And we figure out the next line pretty quickly:

Speak thrice to conjure nothing on the spot.

But the next one is really hard. We get parts of it, but we're missing key words.

Adam reads, "*Who* blanks *here will present be* blank."

I squint at the line. "Banters? Barters?"

"I think that's an *h*. Oh, and that's a *k*. See?"

He's right.

"So . . ." I try again. "Hankers?"

"Harkens!" Adam declares.

"Yes!"

"*Who harkens here will present be* . . . uh, forged?" Adam puzzles.

"The first two lines rhyme," I point out. "So, if these ones do too, then the word has to rhyme with *spot*."

"*Forgot!*" we say together in triumph.

"*Who harkens here will present be forgot*," Adam reads. "What do you think he means by harkens?"

"He Shakespeare?" I ask. "We don't know if—"

Adam lights up. "I know! It's like 'Hark, who goes there?'"

"Maybe, but what does *hark* mean?" I scramble off the bed and type *harken* into the dictionary on my laptop. "Listen," I report. "It means 'listen.'"

"So the person who listens will be forgotten?" Adam asks.

"I guess so."

"Read the whole thing," he says.

I sit up and read what we have so far:

> Ah, treble words of absence spoken low;
> For ears of fam'ly, friend, or willful foe.
> Speak thrice to conjure nothing on the spot.
> Who harkens here will present be forgot.

The words hang in the room.

"Any clue what it means?" Adam asks.

"Nope."

"Okay," he sighs. "What's next?"

"There's a lot of repetition in the last two lines. Look, there are three *ands,* and that word and that one both repeat three times too." I point to two different words, one short, the other longer, neither immediately legible.

"*Treble words . . .*" Adam says. "*Speak thrice,* which also means three. It's saying to repeat something three times, and now the last two lines are the something, and it's repeated three times. Treble. Thrice. Just like it says!"

"You must be right." I grin at him. "So what's the something? Is that a *V*?"

"I think so," he nods. "And an *n*? No, an *o-i*, right?"

"Yeah." I've got it. "It's *void*."

"Yes! Void and nothing?" he suggests.

"Constance said that," I remember. "*Void and nothing. Void and nothing.* It repeats. And then a dash, and . . ."

"*All . . . strife.*"

"That's it! We're so close!"

Adam squints at the last line. "*Third's the* . . ."

"*Charm,*" I read.

Adam nods. "And then it repeats again, *To void and nothing* . . ."

We read the last words together: "*Turn life.*"

"So the last two lines are . . ." We read them aloud.

> Void and nothing. Void and nothing—all strife!
> Third's the charm. To void and nothing turn life.

I shudder. "What does it mean to turn void and nothing into life? It sounds kind of awful."

"Maybe the sentence is sort of backwards." Adam studies the graph paper. "It could mean to turn life into void and nothing."

"That's worse!" I exclaim. "Is it about killing someone? That's what turning life into nothing would be, right?"

"I don't think so." He looks at me. "It's a poem, right, so it doesn't have to mean exactly what it says. I think it's a spell—"

"Adam—"

"No. Let me finish. I think it's a spell, and when you say it, it makes something disappear. That's what happened to the words in the book. They disappeared. Because of the spell."

"But—"

"Conjure!" He hurls the word at me. "*Conjure* means a spell!"

"But you said yourself . . . it's a poem, so it doesn't mean exactly what it says."

I never imagined that I'd be the person in the story who doubts the magic. I reach deep inside myself and grasp on to a fragment of belief.

"The writing did disappear," I concede.

"Right!" Adam sits up. "And maybe the poem somehow made the writing go into void and nothing. Maybe the book isn't magic. Maybe the words are."

"Maybe."

So much of what I've read has prepared me for this moment, but still, I can't quite believe.

We walk downstairs in silence. He says lightly,

"It's supposed to be really warm this weekend. Shelby thought maybe we could go to the island on Sunday."

"That would be great!" I gush. And it would be. No creepy books. Just the boat and the ruins and the Rosie patch and Adam and Shelby and me.

I clomp slowly up the stairs. Emily Dickinson chirps at me, "I dwell in Possibility." Good for her, but it seems I dwell in Doubt.

"Everything okay?" Mom calls from her room down the hall.

"Yeah." I force a cheerful tone, but . . . maybe . . . "Mom?"

I stride down the corridor. She sits in the rocking chair in the corner, a book in her lap.

"Do you know anything about Shakespeare and, like, um, magic spells or anything?" I ask.

She closes her book. "That's precisely the subject Arthur Brooke worked on. Maybe you know that already. From your research on Constance?"

"Yeah." I didn't know, but now I do. "But isn't that, you know, kind of a stupid idea?" I sit on the edge of her bed.

"Well, of course, but scholars have put forward some evidence that Shakespeare may have been using words that others believed to be magic. The best example is in *Macbeth*. You haven't read that one yet, I don't think."

I shake my head.

"Well, there are three witches who make a prediction about what will happen to Macbeth, and it seems like it couldn't possibly come true, but then the words don't quite mean what he'd understood them to mean, and they do come true in a different way," she explains. "So the theory is that the magic words the witches speak—*Double, double toil and trouble; Fire, burn, and cauldron, bubble*—are actually magical. And, they say, that's the reason productions of *Macbeth* are cursed."

"What do you mean, cursed?" I ask.

"Oh, there are accidents, peculiar injuries. There have even been some deaths," she answers.

"Then why did you say the spell?"

"Don't be silly, Rosemary." She laughs. "It's just a superstition. More like a hoax. You know perfectly well there is no such thing as a magic spell."

The diary in the cupboard. The vanished words. *To void and nothing* . . . There is such a thing. Adam's right. Belief vanquishes doubt.

Mom goes on. "Anyway, Arthur Brooke started with the *Macbeth* idea and went looking for other spells in other plays and also in the sonnets. He claimed to find several examples, although when pressed to offer proof, he never had much to show for all his labor."

"Huh. Okay. Thanks."

"Maybe you could use the theory in your project," she suggests.

"Maybe," I murmur. I slide off her bed and head back to my room.

"You have plans for the weekend?" she calls after me.

"Adam and I are going to the island," I answer. "Shelby, too. I mean, Michelle."

"Oh, good. I don't like you two going on your own. The river's unpredictable this time of year."

I don't point out that Shelby's what's unpredictable. And also magic. And words, too, it turns out.

I call Adam.

He answers halfway through the first ring. "Sorry, Rosie, I—"

"No. I'm sorry," I cut in. "I think you're right. It's a spell."

Seven

ADAM AND I don't know how to move forward, or don't want to, so we actually work on the poetry project. Hunkered in my room, we skim the book I got, along with a couple from the library, looking for poems about memory or houses or ruins. It turns out that "Moon Mangled Memory" and "Sifting Words" are in every book of Constance's that we read. In fact, a footnote explains that Constance insisted the two poems appear together in all of her collections.

Each of us tries writing a poem about a house. Adam writes about the cupboard in my room, and I make him tear it up, and he's mad at me, but only a little, because it was a stupid poem. I write about the ruins on the island, and it's an even stupider poem, so I tear mine up too, in solidarity.

"We suck," he says cheerfully.

"Yup," I agree. "What rhymes with *river*?"

"*Giver*," he offers. "*Liver*."

"Oh, that's good." I laugh. "I love living on the river, I love it from my head right to my liver."

"Brilliant!"

We give up trying to write good poems and pass the afternoon writing the worst poems we can and laughing until we cry. The diary hovers at the edge of my brain, but I avoid looking right at it. Writing bad poetry with Adam is so much easier than figuring out whether or not the codex is false, and before we have a chance to face the thick, yellowed pages, it's gotten dark and Adam has to go home. As he gets ready to leave, we settle our plans for our trip to the island. I can hardly wait.

It's not as warm as it was supposed to be, but it's definitely not mid-December cold. I should have worn a heavier jacket, though, and I wrap my arms around myself and bounce on the balls of my feet. The diary is in a canvas bag slung across my shoulder that smacks my thigh as I bounce.

Shelby and Adam walk toward me. They both have on their heavy winter coats, and Shelby is carrying an extra sweatshirt. I should go get a better coat . . .

"Here!" She tosses me the sweatshirt.

"Don't you—" I start.

"It's for you," she says, heading toward the river. "I figured you'd be cold."

Adam takes in my bag and raises his eyebrows. I give the slightest nod to confirm we're on the same page. In a flash, I see the rest of the day—Shelby and me in the V tree, looking through the diary together. Making the diary part of a group with *Pelagia's Boats* and *The Golden Compass* and *The Giver* and the other books we shared there settles my anxiety, partly because they're all books about kids who overcome impossible situations, but mostly because I love those books.

We fall into our usual roles. While Adam undoes the ropes, I stand in the wooden boat, and Shelby positions herself to launch us into the water.

"One." She braces her hands against the back of the boat.

"Two." Adam hurdles aboard, and I grasp the oars.

"Three." Shelby vaults over the stern.

I pull the oars and guide us across the current. Shelby takes the other set, and we stroke in sync, as if we do this every day, as if there's never been a time when Shelby didn't pick up my call.

The current is slow and careless today, easy to get across.

Our talk is slow and careless too. Shelby's part in the musical. Our poetry project. Other trips to the island.

Shelby's earbuds dangle, forgotten, around her neck. This weird techno-scarf is like a badge of high school. It says, *I could tune you out if I wanted to.* But she doesn't tune us out.

"Is this the first time we've gone in winter?" I ask.

"Maybe it'll look different," Adam says.

"The rosemary might be dead," Shelby warns.

"It grows year-round," I protest. "Constance said her father could grow rosemary at the North Pole."

There's no response to that, and we make the rest of the journey in comfortable silence.

Adam grins at us as he starts to twirl the rope.

Shelby rolls her eyes. "Showoff."

In a flash, Adam lassos his sister.

"Hey!" She squirms to free her arms.

"You said show off," he says. "I thought it was a command."

Only mildly annoyed, she throws the rope back to him. Lazily, like he doesn't even have to try, he tosses it toward our regular anchor, a dead tree, toppled long ago. It falls short.

Shelby laughs. "Ha!"

"I can't believe you missed," I exclaim.

"You guys messed me up," he grumbles, pulling the rope back in. He focuses on his mark this time and hurls the rope in a careful, graceful arc. The loop falls neatly over the limb.

Adam walks along the fallen tree trunk and ties the rope to a sturdy branch.

I climb out, Shelby right behind me. My foot slides off a mucky patch of something green. I pitch toward the water. Shelby grasps my elbow. And I'm steady.

"Let's check on the Rosie patch," she suggests.

We struggle through the tangle of broken branches and thick bushes that marks the perimeter of the island. When the river is fast and when it floods, lots of debris gets hung up here. In the summer, people come often enough that it gets cleared out, but the trash caught in the brush is a reminder that no one comes here this time of year. I pluck a broken Barbie doll from a pile of leaves and sticks. She wears a tattered sparkly pink dress and has leaf fragments in her hair. She has only one leg.

"Look!" I call to Adam and Shelby, who are ahead of me.

"Creepy," Shelby replies.

It seems wrong to leave the Barbie, so I bring her along.

We scramble through the crumbled house, piles of gray stone and low walls. The only substantial thing is a fireplace, which looms over the ruins like a guard. I store the image in my mind for our project. Maybe I'll write a poem about the fireplace resisting the flood and the passage of time. My cupboard that used to be a chimney could go in the same poem. I chant under my breath: *Books in chimney space. Ruined fireplace.*

Past the house, there's a hill. It's not very steep, but it's dotted with pricker bushes, so climbing up is tricky. A thorn jabs me, and I concentrate on moving up the slope without getting stabbed a second time.

Shelby is the first to reach the top. "It's alive!" she exclaims.

"It always is," I point out.

Adam offers me a hand up. "It's weird. It sort of goes against the rules of nature, you know?"

The three of us stand on a narrow dirt ledge and look at the broad patch of rosemary bushes. The needles are a dark green on the top and a lighter, sort of sage color underneath, clustered together like on a Christmas tree. The sharp piney smell fills the air.

Years of visits to the island, years of standing on this ledge and wondering at the rosemary crowd together in my memory. "At some point," I say, "when something is the way it is, it has to stop being weird and, you know, just be."

"Very philosophical." Shelby laughs and strides down a path through the bushes to a tiny clearing.

We sit cross-legged in a tight circle on the ground.

"This was bigger before," Shelby observes as her knee smacks against mine.

"We were smaller," I point out.

The river makes a sound like lazy wind, moving past, carrying the odd bit of something with it. I sit the Barbie between me and Shelby, like she's another person in the circle. Shelby and Adam both smile.

We all watch a hawk circle in the sky. I pluck at some rosemary, rub it between my fingers, and inhale the sharp scent.

Shelby pulls her knees to her chest and leans back, her eyes closed.

I follow her lead. The thin winter sun rests lightly on my cheeks.

Adam nudges me with his knee. He wants me to pull out the diary and show Shelby the poem, I can tell, but just knowing she'll help us make sense of it is enough for now. The layered scent of the rosemary, the gentle brushing sound of the river, the easy warmth on my face. I don't want the moment to end. I store up all these sensations in the place where memories of the island live. I put them on a shelf in my mind beside all the other times with Adam and Shelby. I keep them nearby, just like the books by my bed. The idea that memories and books are similar swirls around me with the warmth of the sun.

The sharp pain of Adam's kneecap emphatically thwacking against my thigh breaks my reverie.

I glare at him, but he's eager to show Shelby the poem, and he looks like a little kid, so I can't be mad.

"I brought the diary," I announce, pulling it from my bag.

Shelby leans forward a little, and her hair sheets down alongside her face. As if on cue, her cell phone pings, but she ignores it. She looks expectantly from me to Adam. "Well?"

This is what Adam and I were waiting for. It wasn't that we didn't want to think about the poem; it was that we didn't want to think about it without Shelby.

"So, we told you we found the book in the cupboard," I begin.

"And we took it to use for our poetry journal." Adam speaks firmly, glossing over whether or not writing in the book had been the right decision.

"Mr. Cates said to use Shakespeare for inspiration," I tell Shelby. "So, I wrote the line from *Hamlet* that my name comes from—*Rosemary, that's for remembrance. Pray, love, remember*—and then we realized there was actually writing on the page."

"What did it say?" she asks.

The name bursts into my head like a bright light that suddenly floods the darkness. *Wilkie Wilkie Wilkie Wilkie.*

Adam and I say the name together. Why couldn't we remember it before?

"It said something about how her father told her to write to remember Wilkie," Adam recalls.

Yes. That's what it said. The words clarify in my mind, like a picture coming into focus.

"So we went to see Constance, to ask her about Wilkie." I had lost track of why we went. It wasn't really for the project. It was for Wilkie. But she didn't tell us about Wilkie.

"She has Alzheimer's," Adam says. "She doesn't remember most of her own life, so she didn't remember him."

"That's so sad!" Shelby hugs her knees.

"But then"—I try to put the next piece in place —"the writing was gone. Like it was erased from the book."

"Or it was never there in the first place," Adam adds.

"Is it there now?" Shelby asks.

We all stare at the diary.

I set the book in the dry leaves in front of me and turn the heavy, stiff pages until I come to my own handwriting. The rosemary line at the top of a page filled with Constance's frantic cursive.

Shelby takes the book and stares at the writing, crinkling her nose as she tries to make sense of the looping letters. She turns a few pages. "You say all this disappeared?" I hear the doubt in her voice.

"I know it doesn't make any sense." Adam argues against her skepticism and his own.

"I'm not really sure what happened," I confess.

Shelby reads aloud, slowly, haltingly.

Father thinks Shakespeare actually did magic or, rather, that he borrowed magic. Magic! Who believes in such nonsense?

Shelby leans away from the book. "So she wrote about magic, and you guys are playing it's real?"

It's like she slapped me. The bright red spots in Adam's cheeks mean he feels the same way.

"We're not playing," I say.

"The words really do come and go," Adam insists. He's pulled the graph paper out of his pocket and clutches it as if anything on graph paper has to be true.

"Okay. Okay." She leans in again, the book still in front of her. "I believe there's something weird going on, or at least you both think there is."

That'll just have to do until she sees it for herself. I didn't believe it either. Why should she?

She reads aloud:

I've taken the codex! If father doesn't have the book, this horrible false thing, then he will come back to Wilkie and me. And it is false! There's nothing here except a list of herbs and a poem, and Shakespeare hardly invented herbs, or poetry, for that matter. It's like saying there is a bear in a Shakespeare play, and here is a bear, and therefore it must be Shakespeare's bear. Ridiculous!

"The bear!" Adam echoes. "Shc said that same thing to us at River House."

"So where's the poem?" Shelby asks.

I lean over the book. Like Constance's, my hands know the way. I feel the thickness of the folded page before I see it. I unfold the parchment and sit back so Shelby can see the poem.

Her nose crinkles again. "You can read this? Is it even English?"

"It took a long time to figure out," I explain. "Like, hours."

"I'm sure." She looks up, from me to Adam. "Well? What does it say?"

We look at each other and recite. As we end with "*To void and nothing turn life,*" something flutters in my peripheral vision. The hawk? A sudden ache tugs at my stomach.

"Guys . . ." Panic swoops down and makes me dizzy. "Something's wrong . . ."

Adam stares, but not at me. His eyes widen, and he lunges toward Shelby, or where Shelby was. Now there's nothing there. No one.

Adam and I and the broken Barbie with her frozen smile sit in a circle, and there's a horrible gap. Shelby is gone.

Eight

ADAM SORT OF collapses in mid-lunge and leans awkwardly on his forearms. "What happened?"

The stomach pain is gone as quickly as it came, and my mind staggers through a strange fog. "I don't . . ." I rub my hand over my mouth. The sharp smell of rosemary rises off my fingers. "Shelby!" I cry.

"Shelby?" Adam frowns. Then horror splashes across his face. He leaps up. Steps on the Barbie, who stares out, still smiling, from between his shoe and the dried leaves on the ground.

"Shelby!" he calls, his hand above his eyes as he surveys the island. "Where'd she go?"

"She was just here." It's impossible that she could be anywhere but right here with us. I stand with him and look out over the rosemary patch. The crumbled ruins. A glimpse of the riverbank, almost visible through the thick perimeter of bushes. I turn back, expecting to see Shelby crouched behind Adam in the rosemary, a finger raised to her lips, mischief lighting her eyes, but she's not there.

Adam's arms hang awkwardly as if he was reaching for something but has forgotten what. His cheeks are flushed. "What happened?"

My hand hovers near my mouth. The smell of the rosemary mingles with an acrid something that must be fear.

"Shelby," I whisper. "She disappeared."

My senses can't reach past the weird feeling of the world knocked off its axis. My eyes can't focus. My ears fill with the roar of silence. My fingertips are numb.

I clench my fists at my sides. Breathe in the pungent smell of decaying leaves and sleeping soil.

The fog drifts away, and the weird fear goes with it.

Adam looks more confused than panicked now.

"You okay?" I ask.

He rubs a hand vigorously over his forehead. "I feel really weird. What were we . . . ?"

The metallic taste of blood blooms from the inside of my cheek. I've bitten it again. I press my hand to my face. Shelby's long hair floats to the surface of my memory. "Shelby," I say. "Or is it Michelle?"

Adam is blank. "Sorry. Who?"

"Not funny, Adam." I hug myself against a sudden biting cold.

His eyebrows arch. He seems to think I'm making

a joke that he doesn't get, and he's half waiting for me to explain and half pretending it's funny.

"Shelby," I say again. I have to force out the word, and the shape of it is clumsy in my mouth. For a second, I don't know why I said it, but then I do. "Shelby!" I shout.

"Who the heck is Shelby?" Adam follows my panicked gaze around the island. "No one else is here, Rosie."

"But—" I can't quite get my breath. We came here with Shelby. Michelle Steiner. Sixteen years old. Hands at ten and two on the steering wheel. Leaning towers of books. The V tree. Rowing the boat. My friend. "Your sister?" I whisper, and I can't keep the question out of my voice.

Adam barks out a single laugh, and it makes me wince. "I don't have a sister."

I shiver in that whole-body, someone-walked-over-my-grave way.

He notices. "You're cold. Let's go home."

I pull the sweatshirt tightly against the damp chill. Adam was right. I needed an extra layer.

Did Adam bring the sweatshirt?

I search his face. The soft blue-gray of his eyes is calm, untroubled, like still water.

"Come on, Rosie." Adam starts back to the boat. He walks along the low, ruined wall like it's a balance beam. Picks up a hard green walnut. Shouts, "Incoming!" and chucks the nut in my direction.

I watch it land next to me. I try to see through the fog in my head.

Adam unties the boat, like he always does. I get in and grip the oars. He shoves off and jumps in at once. He takes the other set of oars and sings loudly in made-up Italian.

As we push through the current, a cold rain starts. A drop plops on my cheek.

I let go of the oar to wipe the rain away. My hand still smells like rosemary. From the patch. The Rosie patch. Shelby!

"Adam!" I twist around to look at him. "Where's Shelby? How'd we forget? What—"

The current snatches my oar.

"No!"

I hurl myself to the edge of the boat and grasp the wooden handle just before it escapes my reach. My hands plunge into the water. The day may be unseasonably warm, but the water is frigid. I wedge the oar under my arm and vigorously rub my hands on my sweatshirt. Rub them dry and warm.

Adam sings again. I paddle. Wipe another raindrop from my nose with the back of my hand. This time I keep my grip on the oar. My hand smells like rotting leaves and mud.

"The river stinks!" I call over my shoulder.

"La riverio is estinkio!" Adam sings.

I laugh. "Adamini is estinkini!"

"Rosa Maria is a-stinky like—"

"Shut up!" I giggle.

It's raining hard by the time we get to the bank, and Adam ties the boat quickly while I hop from one foot to the other.

We run through the rain and are soaked to the skin when we get to Adam's house. We burst in the front door, laughing.

"Gracious!" Mrs. Steiner exclaims, stepping back from us and the puddle seeping into her carpet. "Adam!" she scolds. "Get out of those wet clothes! And find something of yours Rosemary can change into."

A thought tries to catch in my brain. Something about clothes I could change into. Not Adam's, but . . . certainly not Mrs. Steiner's.

I trot after him up to his room and take the sweats he tosses me to the bathroom. They're a little too big, but soft and warm, and I'm content as I hang my wet things on the edge of the tub and towel dry my hair. I grin at Adam's toothbrush, sitting in the left hand of a ceramic gnome hunched next to the sink. The other hand is empty.

I turn off the bathroom light. Stop in the doorway.

Adam stands across the hall in front of the guest room. He's silhouetted in the gray light coming from the window. He stands very still. Staring into the empty room.

The off-white bedspread, the off-white walls, the framed print that someone gave the Steiners but no one really likes, the low chest at the foot of the bed where they keep the extra blankets we always used to make forts. Adam and . . . I. We made the forts. The two of us.

The blandness of the room in front of me is sad, like a blank page. No, like an erased page. A memory tries to surface, but something hard and cruel holds it down.

The emptiness of the room is terrible and wrong.

I swallow the knot that rises in my throat.

Adam's eyes catch at mine. "What did we do?"

I don't know. I don't know what we did. We did something. Didn't we? Did we?

"I don't know," I moan. "But something's wrong."

"Isn't it?" He stares at me, desperate. His arm rises weakly toward the guest room. "It's too . . . it shouldn't be . . ."

"It shouldn't be empty," I offer.

He stares at me. "But what . . . not what, who. Who should be in there?"

"The diary . . ." I grope through confusion. "Maybe the diary did it."

He looks defeated.

I take his arm and lead him to his room. Pick up my bag from the floor. Pull out the diary. A streak of damp dashes across the burgundy leather. I wipe it with my palm, and the leather darkens as the water soaks in. I wonder if the cover could actually be skin. I guess that's what leather is, after all. The thought troubles me, and the book looks menacing.

I sit on the floor with my knees pulled up to my chest, a sort of shield against whatever lurks in the book. I reach awkwardly past myself and open the cover. *Constance Brooke, Rosemary Bennett, Adam Steiner.* Seeing our names there, with Constance's, makes me feel uneasy, like the ground beneath me is unstable. And also something else . . . My name there, like I own this book, like I own what it does, fills me with a horrible, sickening guilt. All I want is to hide the book away. Get it out of sight. Shut the guilt up and lock it away and never, ever let it go free.

But I have to turn the page. I have to understand what's happening.

The parchment is thick between my fingers. *Sage, hyssop, chamomile, lemon balm . . .*

Adam still stands, his hands dangling uselessly at his sides.

"Sit," I plead.

He looks around helplessly.

"Adam!"

He struggles to focus on me.

Did we eat something weird? I had that stomach pain. Now I'm achy. Maybe we're sick.

The real-world-ness of that possibility settles me. Gives me something solid to get my head around. "Adam, sit with me." My voice is calm and sure.

He crumples beside me, an awkward sprawl of limbs.

"Here's the list," I say, a little too loudly.

He reaches out and aimlessly turns the page. He fingers the bookmark he made for me and reads my writing, the line from *Hamlet*.

His whole body tenses. "Remember," he repeats.

Giggling in a blanket fort. An arm steadying me from behind. A sheet of blond hair.

"The Rosie patch," I murmur.

"Shelby." Adam mouths the name. And then says it out loud, "Shelby."

"Shelby," I repeat.

"Where did she go?" His voice is high, panicky.

The girl with the blond hair goes blurry around the edges like she's dissolving. All I can picture is that horrible Barbie. Her eyes too blue. Her false smile.

"Rosemary!" Adam shakes me. "Where did she go?"

When he says my name, Shelby snaps into focus. I

grasp at the idea of her like it's a person dangling off a cliff. Slipping. Hang on!

"We all went to the island together." He stands and paces. "You and she rowed. I did the ropes. We went to the rosemary patch."

He stops. Ferociously rubs at his forehead with the palm of his hand.

"We told her about the disappearing writing in the book," I say. The words taste like a lie, but they're not. I know they're not.

"Yes!" Adam seizes the memory of the conversation. "And we showed her some stuff Constance wrote and then . . ."

"And then she wasn't there anymore," I finish.

"Was she ever there?" he asks. A tear falls down his cheek and clings to his jaw. I want to brush it away, but I'm too busy hanging on to the blond girl. The one who . . . the one with . . . like a sigh, she goes.

"What was her name?" Adam asks.

"Barbie?" I toss over my shoulder as I close the diary and put it back in my bag.

"Duh," Adam grumbles. "That's not what I meant . . ."

Something needs to be said, but neither of us knows what it is.

I go home wearing his sweats, with my damp

clothes in a tight bundle that I carry in the crook of my arm. I have that nagging feeling you get when you go on a trip and forget to pack something. I have my clothes. The canvas bag with the diary thumps against my leg as I walk. Nope, nothing is missing.

I lie in bed and listen to the rain. Hard, heavy, insistent. I can't get comfortable. I toss from side to side and turn over and back again. Finally, I give up and reach to turn on the light. I pull the diary off my shelf, and something swirls to the floor. I lean over the edge of the bed and spot the bookmark. The rosemary branches braided around a gold ribbon. I pick it up.

The dry smoothness of the needles reminds me of Shelby.

Shelby! I shoot out of bed and hurry to the door. I have to tell Adam! My hand is on the knob, but it's the middle of the night. It's too late to go over there or even to call, but I can't forget again. I snatch up the diary and grab a pen from my desk.

I hunch on the floor, the book open in front of me.

I turn to a blank page. A blank page like a promise. A promise of not forgetting.

I write fast. *We need to remember Shelby.* And then I write it again. And again. And again. *Shelby. Shelby. Shelby. Shelby. Shelby. Shelby. Shelby. Shelby.*

Tears fall onto the page, fast like the rain, and the

ink blurs, and a sob rises, and I close my eyes and try to hang on to my friend, but she slips from my grasp. And when I open my eyes, I don't know why I'm sitting on my floor in the middle of the night sobbing over a blank page.

Nine

I WAIT OUTSIDE SCHOOL under the overhang, watching the occasional raindrop plop into a puddle nearby, vaguely worrying that I've somehow missed Adam. I guess we could work on the project separately and put our parts together at the end. That might be easier. A bad mood stalks me.

At lunch, Miranda and Kendall chattered about some stupid drama between Hannah and Isabella. I pretended to listen, but I was distracted watching Adam, two tables over, goofing off with Micah and Josh. As usual, Adam had his chef salad ridiculously separated into the different compartments of his tray.

"Rosemary!" Miranda actually snapped her fingers in my face.

"Sorry, what?"

"Hannah told Isabella that Claire . . ."

I tried to listen, but instead, I watched Adam pluck a cherry tomato from the tray.

"What is with you?" Kendall glared at me.

"Sorry."

"Why are you staring at Adam?"

Because he's my friend. Because something dangles unfinished between us. "I don't know," I said. "I mean, I'm not."

Since we went to the island, Adam and I have been weird with each other. I think about last year, when we walked in on his parents arguing about money. We silently agreed never to talk about it, and it became this prickly thing that we skirted ever after. Everything about Adam and me seems prickly now.

I planned to sit with him in Mr. Cates's class so we could talk about our project, but the desks were in triangular clusters of three. I couldn't figure out who would take the third spot if I sat with Adam. Kendall and Miranda waved me over, so I sat with them.

Mr. Cates asked Adam to define iambic pentameter, and Kendall snickered when he gave a perfect definition—ten syllables, in an alternating pattern of unstressed and stressed syllables—and I was proud of Adam for knowing. Kendall tried to catch my eye, but I didn't want to be complicit in the snicker, so I dropped my pencil and rested my hand on the cool tile floor for a few seconds before I picked it up, but it didn't help me pull myself together, because since when have I avoided siding with Adam?

Finally, he bursts out of the school building in mid-laugh, and his bark echoes in the concrete space. He's with Micah, who looks pleased with himself.

Micah stops when he sees me. "Hi, Rosemary."

Adam's smile dims, though his laugh still echoes around us. "Hey, Rosie."

He's not happy to see me.

I swallow pride and confusion. "I thought we better work—"

Adam finishes my sentence. "On our project."

"Yeah." I look from him to Micah. "Are you free?"

"It's okay," Micah assures him.

The three of us walk together, huddled against the rain, which is falling steadily now. Micah turns right, and Adam and I continue in silence.

Being awkward with him is like being awkward with myself. I have to say something. "Did you write more poems? For the project?" I blurt out. "I liked the one about the cupboard."

"You made me tear it up," he reminds me.

"Yeah." I don't know what else to say.

"It wasn't any good, though, so it's okay," he assures me, and the kindness in his tone makes the silence more comfortable.

We stride together through the sloppy, cold rain. Even though he's taller than me, our steps are in sync. We part around a puddle, but step back together.

Adam says, "I was thinking maybe we should focus our project on Alzheimer's."

"Alzheimer's?"

He pushes his soaked hair off his forehead, so it stands up in dark blond spikes. "Some of Constance's poems are about memory, like the moon one, you know, souvenir is lost, or whatever. And now she has actually lost her memory, so I thought . . . yeah."

"The diary . . ." I begin. I want to make a connection between the diary and forgetting, but I can't get the pieces to link up in my head. I focus on Adam. Adam who has been my best friend longer than I can remember. I love the way he eats his salad!

"Alzheimer's is a great idea," I gush. "I mean, it's a terrible idea, but for the project, it's great. As a topic. You know what I mean."

He knows. Whatever was between us has moved out of the way. I tell him about how Kendall and Miranda have switched their poet four times, and Adam complains about the last problem on our math test, and we remember how soaking we were when we came back from the island, and I say, "I need to give you back your clothes."

And for a heartbeat, I'm embarrassed, but then we're laughing, and everything's fine.

"Maybe we should go see Constance again today,"

Adam suggests. "And pay more attention to the Alzheimer's part."

"Sure," I agree. "My mom'll take us. She'll love that we want her help."

"Yeah, okay." He smiles. "And after, we can write about it."

So we have a plan for getting our project done. A good plan. Way better than Googling our poet, or whatever the other pairs are doing. But isn't there something else we want from Constance? A thought tries to gain purchase but slips away. I don't mind, because after that totally inexplicable weirdness, I have my best friend back.

It's really pouring now, and Mom leans forward, struggling to see the road. Slush mixes in with the rain, gliding just out of the windshield wipers' frantic reach.

"This is turning to snow," Mom grumbles as she pulls in front of River House. "I'll just return these library books and be back in half an hour, before the roads get slippery."

We dash through the pelting slush into the flowered lobby. We don't bother with the sunroom this time, but as we hurry past, the wheelchair man in the doorway reaches out a bony arm.

"Maud?" he cries.

"No, sorry," I squeak as I skirt him.

Constance's door is open, and she sits in front of the window, framed by the winter light. She has the black headband on again, but she's wearing a different outfit. A dark green dress with buttons up the front.

"Hello." She smiles, her paper cheeks crinkling. "Do I know you?"

"I'm Adam. This is Rosemary. We came last week." Adam opens a spiral notebook filled with graph paper. "We're working on a project. For school."

"About poetry and memory," I add. "We picked you as our poet."

Her look is polite and bland. She doesn't seem to understand.

"You wrote some poems about memory," Adam reminds her. "Like, uh, the one about the daughter looking out over the river, and also one about a ruined house and how it still holds all the memories from before it was ruined."

"Good job remembering the titles," I say under my breath.

He glares at me. "Do *you* remember them?"

I fish the thin volume of Constance's early poems out of my bag. Constance watches me with mild interest.

I hold the book out to her, and she squints at the

photograph on the cover. Her brow collapses into deep furrows. "Do I know that woman?"

She doesn't recognize herself.

"That's you," Adam answers, his voice gentle.

She smiles uncertainly. She takes in a breath, the start of a laugh that doesn't follow, then catches herself with her mouth open and quickly presses her lips together in a pale line.

I find "Moon Mangled Memory" in the book and read the first verse out loud. "Do you remember this one?" I ask.

Her smile is detached. "No, I'm afraid I don't know that poem. I won the recitation prize in the third grade for Wordsworth's 'I Wandered Lonely as a Cloud.' Do you know it? Shall I say it for you?"

She clasps her hands together like a schoolgirl and begins:

> I wandered lonely as a cloud
> that floats on high o'er . . .

I recognize the words. "That's one of Mr. Cates's poems of the day."

Constance frowns and wrings her hands. "*I wandered lonely* . . . I can't . . ." She looks up as if she might find the words written in the air.

"She doesn't remember that she wrote the moon poem," I murmur.

"Constance." Adam pulls her attention to him. "You were a poet, like Wordsworth. Do you remember?"

She nods solemnly. "Father says I am quite the poet."

"You wrote this book." I hold it up again. "*We mark time by the moon*. You wrote that. Do you remember?"

Constance hugs herself and says softly, "The new moon."

"That's right!" I congratulate her. "That's in the next verse: *The new moon is nothing.*"

"Nothing and everything." Constance fingers a button at her waist.

"Does it say that?" Adam asks, reading over my shoulder.

"No . . . I'll try a different poem." I flip ahead to one called "Dead Echo" and read:

> Listen to the stones that have no voice
> Only silence echoes back my choice

"Constance? You wrote that. Do you remember?"

She smiles. "Hello. Do I know you?"

"He's Adam. I'm Rosemary. We came last week, and you told us about the false codex."

"Did I?" She frowns. "I hate that horrible book. A nasty thing. Full of nothing." She clutches the button now, and the fabric of her dress puckers at her waist.

"*Void and nothing,*" I quote.

Her head whips back like I slapped her. The button snaps off her dress. "What did you say?"

"It—it's from, uh, a poem. It was in the diary. I mean, the codex," I stammer.

"It conjures," she whispers.

"Yeah, the poem has *conjure* in it." I sit forward.

"It conjures nothing." Her hands are idle on her lap now. Her dress gapes where she pulled the button off.

"Nothing," Adam echoes. His gaze darts around the room.

"What's wrong with you?" I hiss.

"That poem . . ." he begins. "The void poem . . ."

"You too?" Constance whispers.

Adam twists the notebook. The metal spiral detaches from the paper and pokes out.

I blaze ahead. "We wanted to talk to you about memory."

"Would you care for some candy?" Constance gestures toward the dish.

"No, thank you," I reply.

She frowns at the button in her hand.

"We should go," I whisper. "This is just sad."

Constance smiles. "Hello. Do I know you?"

"This is Adam. I'm Rosemary."

She nods. "Yes. That's right. Father is magical with rosemary. Truly. Have you seen the patch on the island? He says he could grow rosemary at the North Pole if given the chance, and I think he could. I do!"

She thinks he's still alive. She doesn't remember the poems she wrote because she doesn't remember that she grew up and lived a whole lifetime.

The patter of the freezing rain suddenly quiets, and outside, heavy snow drops past the window. "It's snowing," I point out.

"So it is!" Her face lights up. "Do have a candy," she urges, as if snow demands a celebration.

I take a cellophane-wrapped peppermint.

In the dish, a slip of paper curls, released when I removed the battered old candy. I unfurl it, and there the phrase is again: *Rosemary, that's for remembrance.*

I call her away from the window. "Constance, why do you have this?"

I thrust the slip of paper into her hand. It shakes in her frail claw. She whispers the words aloud. "*Pray, love, remember.*" She looks up, but not at me. "Wilkie." She's pleading with him to stay, with her memory to hold on to him. A tear meanders along the wrinkles etched in her cheek.

"Shelby," Adam whispers. "Michelle?"

Shelby emerges from a fog in my head. She draws

a map of a made-up island country called Marat. She shows me how there are two rivers and when they flood, they join together. I point out how the two branches look like the V tree, and Shelby laughs. "You're right, Rosie!" The fog rises. I clutch at Shelby. At her map. Her laugh, faint and fading.

The silence in the room presses against me.

Constance releases the scrap of paper. It drifts to the ground, keeping pace with the snow falling outside. She twists her black headband, and her eyes move slowly from her own hands to Adam's. She gazes at the notebook screwed up in his hands.

She raises her eyes to his face. "Hello. I'm Constance. Do I know you?"

"No," I snap. "You don't."

"Rosemary!" she cries suddenly.

I'm shocked and flattered that she finally remembers my name.

"You need the other one," she whimpers, and then she shouts, "Rosemary is not enough!"

And from down the hall, the wheelchair man answers, "But you're not Maud!"

She doesn't mean me. Of course she doesn't. These people are all lost in the nonsense of their failing brains. I never, ever want to lose my mind, but something nags at me, something I've forgotten. Maybe I'm already losing my mind.

I pull on Adam's sleeve. "My mom'll be waiting."

He nods, defeated.

"Goodbye. Thanks," I say. "We'll bring you the poems that we write."

She smiles like I said something friendly sounding in a foreign language. "Yes. Yes. Poems are a good way to remember."

I go back and kneel in front of her. "To remember what?"

"To remember who?" Adam echoes behind me.

Her mouth opens. No sound comes out. Her eyes catch at something and then go blank. "Why ever are you down there on the floor? Have you lost something?"

I take her hand. It feels like a tissue, like the first one in a new box still pulled tight in the package. "Look, Constance. It's snowing."

"Why, so it is!" She gazes out the window.

I place her hand gently on her lap and look away from the embarrassing gap in her dress. Adam and I slip into the hallway and walk in silence through the too-bright corridor.

The automatic glass doors seal behind us.

"It's worse than dying." Adam forces his voice to be steady. "Dying is the end of life, but Alzheimer's undoes life, like the life never even happened." His voice is muffled by the blankness of the snow.

"Her poems are a record of her life," I point out.

"But she doesn't know that."

I try to hold on to what Constance said. "What do you think she meant about rosemary isn't enough and we need the other one?"

He shakes his head, grief tugging at his face. A snowflake drifts onto his eyelashes and clings there for less than a second before dissolving to nothing.

Ten

ADAM AND I sit on my bed, trying to organize what we know.

"The poem is the only thing that stays in the codex," I say.

"And the list," Adam adds. "And the stuff we wrote."

"But the poem is the problem. The void . . . It's dangerous."

"Read it," Adam suggests.

I unfold the page and speak the strange verse:

> Ah, treble words of absence spoken low;
> For ears of fam'ly, friend, or willful foe.
> Speak thrice to conjure nothing on the spot.
> Who harkens here will present be forgot.

I don't say the last two lines out loud. The snow falls outside, and it softens the night, like the universe sighing with relief.

"If it's a spell," Adam begins, "then it seems like those first four lines are sort of an introduction. Because it says about speaking three times for the ears of family, friend, or foe, and then the last two lines are what you speak."

"Void and nothing," I say. The phrase begins strong and glaring with the harsh *oi* sound in *void* and then trails away into the softer sounds of *nothing.* I remember Mr. Cates talking about sound in poems, the words performing what they describe.

Then Adam says the thing that's been resolving into clarity ever since we followed Constance's skeletal hands to the folded page. "The poem makes the person listening disappear. Constance said what it does, but we didn't understand. She said it conjures nothing."

"It sends people into the void. It makes them disappear even from memory," I add, and a raw feeling of panic rushes into the space left by someone I've forgotten.

"Do you think that's why Constance has Alzheimer's?" Adam asks.

"Lots of people have Alzheimer's," I answer. "The poem is supernatural, and Alzheimer's is, you know, biological. Constance is the victim of both."

"It's not fair," Adam says.

"No," I agree. The wheelchair man who wants

Maud, Anna and the Hello Kitty lady with their cards scattered under the table, Constance with her broken memory . . . none of it is fair.

Adam leans against the wall. "So we know the poem made Constance forget someone, but we don't know who."

"Was it only Constance?" I ask.

"What do you—? We didn't forget anyone . . . or, I guess, I mean . . . did we?" Adam's horrified now. "How would we know?"

"After Constance read the rosemary line from *Hamlet*, she remembered, didn't she?" Gears in my head grind toward the next step.

"You wrote the same line in the codex," Adam remembers.

"And writing appeared!"

Adam recites, "*Rosemary, that's for remembrance. Pray, love, remember.*"

And all in a flash I do. Shelby teaching me how to pirouette, back when she still took dance. Shelby rowing the boat like she was Pelagia saving the world in *Pelagia's Boats.* Shelby not picking up her phone. Shelby. Shelby. Shelby.

Wilkie Wilkie Wilkie staining the page.

Adam sits utterly still. All color has drained from his face. Sweat beads on his upper lip, and his eyes dart. He's remembering too.

"Maybe if we write the line. In the book." He staggers away from forgetting, toward his sister. "*Rosemary, that's for* . . . Shelby!" he sobs.

"Try it." My voice comes out hoarse but hopeful. I shove the book at him. "Maybe the rosemary line is a spell too. Maybe writing it in the book will bring her back."

Adam leans over the codex and writes the remembrance line.

The words sit on the page like a promise. I hold on to Shelby in my memory, but she doesn't magically appear.

"It was a stupid idea," he sighs.

I say the line out loud.

In my mind, Shelby hands me a copy of *When You Reach Me.* "This. Is. The. Best. Book. Ever." She stirs cookie dough and pretends to be Swedish. She lends me a sweatshirt because she knows I'll be cold.

Adam recites facts about Shelby as if they might pull her back from the void. "Michelle Sarah Steiner. Born April twelfth. She hates hard-boiled eggs. She loves the sound of the cello. She used to dance. She was sixteen."

"She *is* sixteen," I protest. "She's not dead."

And we tumble into each other in a messy hug. My forehead presses against his collarbone.

"How do we know?" he whispers into my hair.

The solidness of him grounds me. I pull back from him and grasp his arms. "We would know if she was dead. We would remember that."

I look down at the codex. The page is crowded with words. "Look!"

The writing is cursive, slanted and a little sloppy. Constance's writing.

Adam starts deciphering. He reads aloud with a fierce desperation, underlining the words with his finger.

> *Mother would never have stood for it. That's what Wilkie says. I don't know because I don't remember her. Not much anyway. Just a white dress with a lacy bit that was nice to run my fingers over, and part of a song she used to sing, and how when she got sick they sent me away and then she was dead.*

Adam stops. "This doesn't help. There's no information. Just sadness."

"She doesn't remember her mother," I say. "But she remembers that she's forgotten. I mean, she knows she had a mother."

Adam shifts so he's a little farther from the book. "Still, how can you forget your own mother?"

I shrug and swallow the thickness that gathered

suddenly in my throat. "Constance was little when her mom died. How much do you remember from when you were five?"

"My birthday party at the park, you dropping that heavy bottle on your toes, signing up for the reading program at the library."

"I don't really remember my father," I confess in a low voice.

"That's different." Adam flushes.

"How? How is it different?" The old anger flares up. Kids whose parents die get sympathy and a grieving process. Kids whose parents just wander away get puzzled frowns and question marks.

Adam's gaze softens, but his words are hard. "It's different because your dad chose for you to forget him."

He has actually said the thing no one else has said or will ever say to me. Emptiness stretches all around me, a desert of not having a father that reaches as far as the eye can see.

Constance's mother probably tried desperately to hold on to life, to her children. She would have wanted to stay with them, but was dragged away kicking and screaming by death.

Like my mother would be. The happy warmth of curling up together on a cold day, the companionable banging around in the kitchen, the gleeful thrill of entering a bookstore.

Some people don't deserve to be forgotten. Constance's mother and . . . who else? We weren't upset about her mother or my father. It was something else. Someone else.

I trace Adam's handwriting in the diary, murmuring the words. *Rosemary, that's for* . . .

An image of a Barbie smiling blankly next to the empty space where Shelby had been bursts into my mind. "We said the poem," I remember.

"And it made her go. The poem made Shelby go," Adam says. "Will she come back?"

I can't bring myself to say that I don't know, that I don't understand any of this, that nothing in my life or even in all the books I've read has prepared me for this. I cling to the one bright spark in this hideous dark. "The line from *Hamlet* makes us remember her."

"But she's still gone," Adam cries. "And we keep forgetting. What if we forget and never remember again?"

"Constance said . . ." I struggle to recall her words. "She said, 'You need the other one.'"

"The other what?" Adam wails.

I shake my head. I have no idea.

His hand trembling, Adam slowly turns to the beginning of the book and scrawls *Rosemary, that's for remembrance. Pray, love, remember* on a blank page. He snaps out the words as he writes them. Turns the page. Scrawls. Snaps. Turns. Scrawls. Snaps. Again and again and again. I reach out a hand to calm him, but he doesn't even seem to know I'm here. And on some pages words appear, always in Constance's slanted cursive. He doesn't stop to read them. He just writes around them and recites. Over and over. *Rosemary . . . Pray . . . Remember.*

Then he stops.

"You!" He looks up at me, his eyes red.

What did I do? And then I see. It's my writing on the page. I rise up on my knees to read what I wrote: *We need to remember Shelby. Shelby. Shelby. Shelby. Shelby. Shelby. Shelby. Shelby. Shelby.*

Thoughts pile up quickly. "The codex . . . the answer has to be here."

I turn pages, looking for a clue. Until I come to a page only half filled with writing. The words stop suddenly just past the middle of the page. And the blankness holds the answer. Whatever made Constance stop writing is what we're looking for.

I read quickly, paraphrasing for Adam as I go. "Her father's all haunted and trying to find the book, and she gets him to admit that it can't really be Shakespeare's, that it's a false codex, but then she feels guilty. She says, *The fragment troubles me.* Do you think that's the poem?" I don't wait for an answer. I keep reading and fear rises into my throat. "She's waiting for Wilkie, and she knows he's coming because she can hear him whistling." My hand flies to my mouth. "She recites the poem."

I bite my lip and read aloud:

I have tried to understand why father believes so absolutely that the fragment is magic. I know it by heart, this verse that has so preoccupied my father. I recite it, and the rhyme drifts over the river and dies.

"That's it. That's all she wrote."

"She disappeared Wilkie," Adam whispers.

"We disappeared Shelby," I say, the horrible truth rising like bile in my throat. "It was us. We're the bad guys."

"The book doesn't say how to fix it." Adam sounds numb now. "She didn't know how. If she did, she would've done it. Wilkie wouldn't be gone."

"We can't give up!" I protest. "Maybe she did know, but she didn't do it right or she ran out of time. Maybe she put the answer someplace else."

"Where?" Adam cries. "We can't sift through all the words in the world."

Sifting words. Constance's poems. "Maybe she put the answer in a poem."

I shove the diary away and grab the volume I got at Eliot Books. The black-and-white Constance on the cover watches me. "Let's start with 'Moon Mangled Memory.' If she wanted it printed in all her books, it must be important."

"Okay," Adam agrees. He sounds defeated. I suspect he would agree if I said "let's stand on our heads," but we need to do *something,* and maybe there will be an answer in the poem.

I read the first line. "*We mark time by the moon.* So, that means how the phases of the moon are a way of telling time, right? The next line is *Our shadow casting dark.*" After the easy clarity of the first line, this one's a puzzle. "Maybe shadows are darker because of the moon?"

"No." Adam sits forward. "I think *our shadow* means the shadow of the Earth. You know, how it's the Earth's shadow on the moon that makes a half moon or a crescent or whatever."

"Yes!" I read on. "*The light left over fills / Our night and lends us sight.* The light that isn't blocked by the Earth's shadow is the moonlight."

"Keep going." Adam looks more hopeful now.

"The next verse is also about the phases of the moon," I say. "It goes through all of them and ends with *A new moon is nothing.* Didn't Constance say something about the new moon?"

"Did she?" Adam cocks his head to one side. "Maybe. Keep reading."

"It kind of elaborates on the idea of the new moon. *A beginning that is / Absence, blankness and void.*"

"The new moon is the beginning?"

"It's the *new* moon, so I guess that makes sense," I say. "But it seems more like an end, if it's absence and blankness . . ."

"And void," Adam and I say together.

A circle of only two people. Absence and blankness.

"The poem," I whisper.

"The poem is the void, or it opens the void," Adam says.

"Maybe the poem is only magic at the new moon?" I suggest.

"But it wasn't the new moon when we went to the island," Adam counters. "Read the last verse."

> A new moon is nothing.
> No light. No sight. Recall
> Only darkness. Absent
> Souvenir. All is lost.

My voice hangs in the room.

"All is lost when souvenir—memory—is absent." Adam works backwards through the lines. "And memory goes dark when the moon dies."

"But we have memory as long as we have the rosemary line."

Adam murmurs the line like a prayer, and I remember Shelby leaning against the V tree, holding a handful of dangling willow branches in her hand.

My own hands go numb as I figure out the piece Constance's "Moon Mangled Memory" adds to the puzzle.

"I think once the new moon comes, the magic is irreversible," I say. "The new moon seals the spell."

"All will be lost." Adam paraphrases the last line.

"But not yet." I grasp at hope and possibility. "How long do we have?"

Adam's thumbs fly as he searches for the answer. He stares at the phone and then at me. "Just three days," he reports.

In my mind, in my unmangled memory, Shelby looks at me steadily, willing me to fix this.

But I don't know how. A sob rises. "All we've learned is that we don't have much time."

Eleven

ADAM STANDS UNDER the streetlight. He holds the rosemary bookmark in one hand and, in the other, a piece of paper with the rosemary verse printed in big letters. Snow falls on his hair, on his shoulders.

"What if I forget?" His face is pinched with worry.

I shiver on the doorstep.

"Rosie!" Mom calls. "Shut the door. It's freezing!"

"You won't," I promise. "Between the actual rosemary and the rosemary spell, you'll remember." I don't add that I'm just making this up or that, not long ago, I was pretty sure the idea of a spell was ridiculous.

He clings to the sprig and the paper. He turns away.

"I'll see you tomorrow," I call after him.

I take the steps two at a time and lunge across my bed to the window. Adam is only a dark shape against the moon-white snow.

Something drops from his hand. The rosemary! I smack my hand against the windowpane. He doesn't hear, but he bends, picks up the tiny branch, shoves his hands with their precious mementos into his pockets, and lopes out of sight.

I study the shape of my face in the bathroom mirror. My broad forehead, wide cheekbones, and pointy chin. The same as Mom's. Maybe Constance looked like her mother. Maybe her mother lived on in that way.

I look for traces of my father in my eyes, the curve of my mouth, the tip of my nose, but I don't find him. I can't find the image of him in my mind.

Mom appears in the doorway and smiles at me in the mirror, but her eyes are sad.

"What?" I ask.

"You're as tall as me now." She leans forward to rest a hand on top of my head.

The warmth and pressure of her touch steady me. "Is that bad?"

"No, but the smaller you is gone, and that's—well, it's just a little bit of a loss. That's all."

I meet her gaze in the mirror. "I don't remember Dad. I mean, I can't picture him."

The hand on my head moves to stroke my hair. She says softly, "Sometimes forgetting is easier."

"How?" I'm not protesting. I'm just asking.

She studies me. "Trying to hang on to what's gone just causes pain. It's better to focus on what we have."

"I have a father." It's a simple statement of fact, but even as I say the words, they strike me as false.

Mom reads my mind. "Not really, Rosie. Not in the way you deserve."

I turn to look at her for real, but even without the mirror, I'm gazing at a reflection. We share the same speckled brown eyes, the same cheekbones, and the same dry lips, chapped from biting them.

I hug her. She hugs back. I want to tell her about the void poem and the new moon, and I want her to help me understand this horrible aching loss at my core, but I don't know the words to describe what's happened.

"Good night, my love." Mom releases me and strokes my hair one more time before padding down the hall to her room.

"Night," I say to her back. I stand for a minute, wanting to say something more, but finding only uneasy silence.

I collapse onto my bed and read Adam's scrawl, angled at the top of a page in the codex. I breathe out the words: *Rosemary, that's for remembrance. Pray, love, remember.*

And memory rises out of the void. Constance and Wilkie and Shelby. I cling to Shelby, wrapping my mind around her, holding her, and lining up memories of books and boats and plays and talking or just sitting not talking. I hold on to her as tightly as I can, but she slips away. I have just space enough in my head to wonder why the spell doesn't summon my father.

I wake to the glorious gift of a snow day, which means it's winter break now. No school for three weeks! And that's an eon of bonus time for our poetry project. I call Adam, but he doesn't pick up. The snow still falls steadily. Mom reports that we may get as much as two feet.

I curl up with a book, one I know well, and reading words I could recite from memory is like snuggling under a warm blanket. Mom is reading too, and we hang out all day in a happy silence, broken only by grilled cheese and tomato soup at lunchtime and tea later in the afternoon.

In the blue of dusk, the snow finally stops. I go to my room and shift the diary off my bed. It opens to a page in the middle. Adam's handwriting. Messy and desperate. *Rosemary, that's for . . .*

I read the whole line out loud, and waves of memory break over me. Shelby and Wilkie and I need to talk to Adam. I can't believe I forgot! And he hasn't called, which can only mean he forgot too. The rosemary and the rhyme weren't enough.

I struggle to steady my shaking fingers enough to call him.

"Yeah?"

"Adam!"

"Hey, Rosie." He couldn't sound more normal. "Isn't this snow awesome?"

"Do you still have the bookmark?" I ask. "Or the paper?"

"Huh?"

"The rosemary," I moan. "The bookmark and the verse. You had them yesterday."

"I did? Sorry. I don't have them. Hey, you want to go sledding tomorrow? Micah and some people are meeting in the morning. At the grove."

"Adam," I beg. "Listen: *Rosemary, that's for remembrance. Pray, love, remember.*"

"Okay." He still sounds completely unconcerned. "That's the *Hamlet* line your mom took your name from. Are we playing Rosie trivia?"

My stomach hardens into a knot. It doesn't work over the phone.

"Please, Adam," I plead. "Will you check your pockets? Please? It's really important."

"For the bookmark? You can get another one," he says, exasperated. "It's no big deal."

He doesn't even remember that he made it for me. That it was a gift. That he picked rosemary in the summer and kept it and pressed it for almost three months. For me.

"But it is a big deal!" Tears blur my vision. "Please. Just look for it."

"Okay. Whatever. I'll look for it later."

"Now!" I sob. "You have to look for it now."

"Jeez, Rosie. What's up with you?"

"It's about Shelby," I whisper.

I already know what he'll say.

"Who?"

"Shelby is your sister," I say firmly, swallowing a sob.

Adam barks a laugh. "I don't have a sister, dork. Is this some sort of joke? It's not actually very funny, Rosie. You're kind of creeping me out."

"Can you come over?" If he hears the verse in person, then he'll remember Shelby. And he'll remember our friendship. "Or I could come there?"

"Nah. My parents are actually home 'cause of the snow, so we're having family game night. Scrabble!"

I screech the rosemary verse at him, willing the spell to do its work over the phone.

"Rosie. Get a grip. You're being really weird."

"Sorry." I can't stand him being so annoyed at me.

"Whatever. You coming sledding tomorrow?" He asks, but he doesn't care whether I come or not.

"Maybe," I manage to croak. "Bye."

I set the phone on my windowsill. Stare at *Shelby Shelby Shelby* in my handwriting in the codex. I make a decision. I tear a page from my spiral notebook and print the *Hamlet* line. I fold it and put it in my pocket.

But like Adam, I'll forget it's there, and it won't do me any good. I have to remember. I cast around my room for something that makes noise. A bell! I tug a jingle bell necklace off a stuffed bear, one that Shelby carefully arranged on my dresser, and shove it in with the paper. The noise will remind me. I hope.

I race down the stairs and tug on my boots. Grab my warmest coat from the closet. Gloves. A hat.

"I'm going to Adam's!" I shout.

"Okay." Mom's voice wafts from the family room, where she's lost in her book. "Call me when you get there."

"Sure." I clomp back to my room, grab my phone, check the time, and jam it into my coat pocket. I walk briskly away from the guilt that prowls behind me.

I turn uphill and tramp through mounting snow to Main Street. Sweat beads along my hairline underneath my wool hat. Maybe this isn't a good idea, but it's the only idea. I have to get there.

It usually takes about five minutes to get to Adam's. I check the time on my phone. Seven minutes. I stop, catch my breath, call Mom.

The pale yellow streetlight catches at the snow crystals.

I hug myself against the cold.

"Hey, I'm here," I lie, sort of.

"Okay. Don't stay too late. Do you want me to walk over and get you in an hour or so?" she asks.

"No! They're playing a game. I may be a while. I'll be fine. Bye."

I put the phone back in my pocket. I wasn't actually lying. I am here. They are playing a game. I may be a while. I don't know about the being fine part. Of course she thought "here" meant Adam's, so basically I did lie. But I didn't have a choice.

I trudge across Main Street and up North Second. It's going to take me almost an hour to get there. The same to get back. I won't have much time.

With each step, the bell in my pocket tinkles. There's paper in my pocket. Paper with a spell on it. A spell in my pocket. A spell in my pocket. The words become a chant that I mutter under my breath as I march through the snow. Four blocks and on to River Road. Here there's no sidewalk, and I have to walk in the road, but there is no traffic. No one is out. No one is out because it's stupid to be out. Dangerous, probably. A spell in my pocket. Trudge. A spell in my pocket.

The lights of the nursing home twinkle into view as I round the curve. I'm nearly there.

They've already plowed the parking lot, and I trot toward the glass doors. The bell tinkles. A spell in my pocket. I pull the wad of notebook paper out. Unfold it. *Rosemary* . . . and memory wells up. Shelby. I'm here for Shelby. And Adam. And myself.

The doors slide open. No one is at the desk. A little plaque says to please sign in, but I don't. I follow the corridor to the sunroom, dim and subdued in the night. Wheelchair man is not there.

Constance's door is shut.

I knock.

No answer.

I can't have come all this way for nothing! Desperation rises up.

I knock again, more of a pound this time.

"Yes?"

I open the door. "Hello, Constance," I peer into the room. The light is off. "I'm sorry. Did I wake you?"

"Oh, no. I turned off the light, the better to look out, you know. If you look out at the night with the light on, you just see yourself reflected back."

I resist the impulse to flick on the light as I enter, and I cross over to the window. She's sitting in the chair, so I perch on the bed. The snow catches light from somewhere and glows in the darkness.

I get right to the point. "The poem makes people disappear."

She doesn't look away from the window. She doesn't respond. Did she hear me?

"Constance." I try again. "The poem. In the codex. It makes people disappear."

"It conjures nothing," she says matter-of-factly.

"Right." I understand those words for the first time. "It makes something into nothing."

"It conjures nothing," she repeats.

"It makes people disappear. Like my friend. Like your brother."

"No. I don't have a brother. Just Father and me. Mother died when I was only five. The flu pandemic, you know."

I say firmly. "You did have a brother. Wilkie. Only the poem disappeared him." I clutch the paper in my pocket and recite, "*Rosemary, that's for remembrance. Pray, love, remember.*"

"Wilkie," Constance murmurs. Delight bursts on her face. She looks around her, and the delight curdles into a frantic, bewildered searching.

"Please," I say. "Isn't there a way to get them back?"

The soft blankness of the snow holds her gaze, and her face reflects the blankness, worry and delight both smoothed away.

"There must be," I insist. "The verse only brings them back on the page and in memory. And then they're gone again. There has to be a . . . like, an antidote."

"Father says we must look in all the plays." Her

voice is small, like a child's. "We don't need to read them. It's just sifting words."

"You wrote a poem called that! Is the answer there? Does your poem say what we need to find?"

She looks steadily at the snow.

"Is it a word? A rhyme? An herb? Constance, what am I looking for?" My face is damp with tears. I don't know when I started to cry.

"I sift words like sand," she says. "Looking for a single grain."

"But that's impossible!"

"That's what everyone always says, but Father is simply magical with rosemary." She settles back in her chair and stretches out her legs a little. "He always says he could grow rosemary at the North Pole if given the chance, and I'm quite sure he could. Quite sure!" Her smile is kind, gentle, but not deep. It doesn't extend to her eyes. She squints at me. "I'm sorry, do I know you?"

"It's funny, actually," I sigh, getting up to go. "My name is Rosemary."

"Ah, then, you may just have a chance." She turns back to the window, and I slip away.

I may have a chance.

I stomp snow from my boots and hurry upstairs to my room, to Constance's book of poems. I have to start sifting.

Mom meets me in the hallway. "How's Adam?"

"Fine," I say, because I'm sure he is. I finger the folded paper in my pocket. He shouldn't be fine. He should be wading through grief and regret, but he's fine because he's forgotten. "We're going sledding tomorrow," I add, shifting my weight from foot to foot, anxious to get into my room.

"You'll have to go in the morning," she says. "It's going to warm up quickly."

"There's, like, two and a half feet of snow out there!" I exclaim.

"Warm air is coming in fast," she says. "With all the rain we had, and the rapid snowmelt, the river will likely flood. So you should go sledding early, while you can."

"Okay," I agree. "Well, good night." I can't stand here chatting about the weather.

"Night, Rosie."

"I love you, Mom."

"I love you too."

I step into my room and gently close the door behind me, careful not to seem to be shutting her out.

The thin book of poems sits on my desk. I find "Sifting Words." It's almost a sonnet. It has thirteen lines, with an eight-line part and then just a five-line part, like she forgot the last line. Maybe she did.

I read the first stanza slowly. It's actually pretty

straightforward, for a poem. She talks about how words make the different parts of a poem:

> Words join up with armies of phrases, lines
> That march on iambic feet, singing rhyme.
> They enjamb boldly, aspire to meaning.

Then it's about the parts of plays, like soliloquys and scenes. The poem is about what Constance described—sifting through the words in Shakespeare's plays—but it doesn't tell me what I'm looking for.

I move on to the second stanza:

> But play, act, scene, speech mean nothing for me.
> Rhyme and meter are immaterial.
> Only words matter. Only one word.
> I rue the day I learned to seek, knowing
> I could never catch a word so well hid.

A hidden word is exactly what I need, but what word? She says "only one word," but she doesn't say what it is. Maybe she didn't know.

Despair flattens me. I crumple back onto my bed. The bell in my pocket tinkles and jars something loose in my mind. I pull out a folded paper and whisper the words written there.

Shelby! Love for Shelby, for Adam, for Mom

vibrates through me, but even love disappears into the void. Love can't fight this awful, grasping forgetting. I hang on to Shelby with all my might and read "Sifting Words" again.

It doesn't have lots of nooks and hidden places like some poems have. It seems to say what it means, but it must have double meanings somewhere. I take the poem's advice and sift the words. I ignore meaning and just look at the letters on the page. *Sift. Words. Armies. Enjamb.*

I stagger from the bed and wake up my laptop. I type *enjamb* into the search box. It means when a sentence carries over from one line of poetry to the next, which I already knew, but maybe it has another meaning as well. The definition includes the phrase "mixed message." That's what I'm looking for. Something that can mean more than one thing.

I scan the poem again, looking for any word I don't know well, or any that might have a double meaning. *Rue?*

I type *rue* on my laptop.

"To feel regret or sorrow." That makes sense. Constance wrote, "I rue the day I learned to seek," which means she regrets that she has to sift words. She regrets losing . . . I struggle for the name . . . Wilkie. She rues his loss, though she doesn't know, in the poem, that she's lost him.

I scroll down to the second definition. *Strong-scented woody herb used for medicinal purposes.*

Shelby nods encouragement.

Wilkie whistles.

Hope dares to sit up.

Rue is an herb.

Twelve

I HESITATE IN FRONT of the cupboard in my room, take a breath, and lift up my father's gigantic *Riverside Shakespeare.* It weighs down my arms with the density of about two thousand hair-thin pages. I turn to the table of contents. There are so many plays!

"Rosie." Mom sticks her head into my room. She registers what I'm holding. "What on earth are you doing with that? Are you reading Shakespeare?"

She's constantly trying to get me to read this play or that one. I can tell she's pleased I'm following her advice, but she wishes I wasn't clutching my father's old book like it's a life preserver. She wants Shakespeare to come from her.

I go for a vague version of the truth. "Constance Brooke said something about one of the plays, so I thought I'd look at them. You know, see if Adam and I want to include some Shakespeare in our project, which won't be due till after Christmas now, because of the snow day, so we have more time, and . . . well, yeah."

She beams at me. "Which play? I have most of them in single volumes, you know. That'd be much easier to read."

"I'm good with this." I hug the *Riverside Shakespeare* to my chest. "It has all the plays in one place, so that seems kind of more efficient."

"But you must have a particular play in mind," she insists.

"There are a couple, actually. I'm just going to kind of browse around for now."

"Okay. I'll leave you to it. But I'm here if you need me." She retreats to her room.

I do need her. She might know where I can find rue, but why am I even looking for references to a random plant? I shake my head to clear the rising fog. What possessed me to drag this enormous volume out of the cupboard? I don't want to read Shakespeare! Certainly not my father's Shakespeare.

I drop the book on my desk with a dull thud and reach for an old favorite instead. Something tinkles in my pocket.

I pull out the old jingle bell necklace from my teddy bear and a piece of paper. *Rosemary, that's for remembrance. Pray, love . . .*

I do! I do remember! Rue. Rosemary and rue. I

have to find the antidote spell. In Shakespeare. I rest my hand on the big book. That's why . . . but I mustn't keep forgetting.

I snatch a pen from my desk and write in thick black ink on the back of my left hand. *Rosemary* . . . It almost doesn't fit, and the last word, *remember,* snakes up my thumb.

As long as I can see my hand, I should remember what I'm doing.

I sit on my bed, the enormous book open in front of me to the first play. *A Comedy of Errors.* It begins with a list of the characters—the *Dramatis Personae.* Then ACT I, Scene I. A stage direction says who enters, and a guy named Egeon gets the first lines:

> Proceed, Solinus, to procure my fall,
> And by the doom of death end woes and all.

Doesn't seem like much of a comedy. Ending woes would be good, but he says death is the way to end woe, which is not so good. I keep reading. A long speech by a duke about merchants and some sort of disagreement. This is going to take forever.

Maybe I don't actually need to read the plays. Like Constance said. I just need to look for the word *rue.* Don't read. Just hunt.

I scan the lines of text, sifting words, not trying to

make sense of what I'm reading. Sense is a distraction. I just need those three letters. *R-U-E.*

A. Heavier. Task. Could. Not. Have. Been. Imposed. The meaning hovers over the words on the page. I have to agree. This is certainly a heavy task. It gives whole new meaning to "Word Search."

Search. Oh! How could I be so dumb?

I grasp my laptop and type *Shakespeare and rue* in the search box.

The first thing that comes up is the definition of rue and then a guide to what different plants mean. Rosemary is associated with memory. Rue with regret. Two different ways of holding on to the past. Regret is like a curdled version of memory.

The next search results are about Ophelia's speech in *Hamlet*, the same one my name comes from but a different part. *There's rue for you, and here's some for me.* Could this be what I'm looking for?

I say the line aloud, but nothing happens.

It turns out there's a bookstore in Paris called Shakespeare & Company, and the word for street in French is *rue*, so a bunch of the results are for the bookstore.

A knock on the door, and Mom hovers awkwardly on the threshold. "Sorry to interrupt," she murmurs. "I just wondered . . . Did you pick one?"

"One what?" I keep clicking, not getting anything useful.

"Play?" She looks at the volume abandoned on my desk.

"Oh, actually . . ." She must know a better way to do this. "I'm trying to find stuff, writing I mean, about rue."

She cocks her head to one side. "Rue? As in regret?"

"Um, yeah. But also, isn't it, like, a plant?"

"It's an ornamental plant. Of course, rue is one of Ophelia's flowers . . ."

"I already found that one."

She smiles at me. "Of course, you know the best part of that speech: *Rosemary, that's for remembrance. Pray, love, remember.*"

Shelby bursts into my brain. She reaches to pluck something from my hair. She puts out an arm to stop me crossing the street as a car speeds through the red light. She and Adam look up at me, their eyes bright, their smiles warm, as I walk into their kitchen.

"Rosemary!" Mom raises her voice. "Goodness, you're lost in your head!"

"Sorry," I mutter.

"Why do you want rue?"

"Constance made a connection between rue and memory," I explain, hoping fiercely that she won't ask me to cite the poem.

She doesn't. She gets all chipper in that my-daughter-is-interested-in-my-world way and says, "You need a concordance."

"A what?"

"A concordance. It's an index to an author's work. A list of each usage of a word."

"Are you kidding?"

She smiles. "Nope."

"Do you have one?" Please say yes. Please say yes.

"Anyone with the internet has one." She leans over me and types *Shakespeare Concordance.*

A site opens up. The portrait of Shakespeare with earrings is there, and on the other side of the screen, a search box waits.

"Wow!" I hold my thumb with the word *remember* against the palm of my hand. I'm close. I'll find it—the antidote spell—I will. *Shelby. Shelby. Shelby.*

Mom stands up, reluctantly. "I don't want to crowd you," she says. "I'm going to take a bath. Tell me what you find."

"Thanks." I'm already typing. *Rue.*

Mom stands in the doorway. "How many?" she asks.

My heart sinks. "Nine hundred forty-two."

Her eyebrows arch. "That's a lot. You need a way to narrow the search."

I sigh.

Mom pads down the hall. Water starts to fill the tub with a roar.

I stroke *remember* on my thumb. *Remember. Shelby.*

Shelby who is Adam's sister. My friend. My mind pushes me toward the past tense: Shelby was Adam's sister. She was my friend. But I hold Shelby in the present tense. She lies in the Rosie patch, her hair puddled around her head in a blond swirl. She looks at the sky, encouraging Adam and me to describe what we see in the clouds. A bee lands on my cheek, and I squeal. She sits up and says, "It's just a bee! You're thousands of times bigger than it." The bee flies away, and I relax into the calm that Shelby creates around us. *Shelby. Shelby. Shelby. Remember.*

I focus on the screen. Number one is from *All's Well That Ends Well*. Just the title brings tears to my eyes.

The text is tight, small. The search term is highlighted in a pale maroon. It says, *true.* Oh! Because *rue* is part of *true*! I page down. *True. True. True.* They're all *trues*! The burden lightens. I just have to look for *rue* in the midst of all the *truth*. How poetic! I smile at myself.

Constance wouldn't have had the internet with its search boxes blinking encouragingly. She would have had thousands of pages of plays. She would have run out of time. She did run out of time.

But I won't. I can't.

Page down. Page down. Page down. There's also *truer* and *untrue.* Page down. Also, *cruel.* And here's *misconstrues.*

Finally, on page eight, here's *rue*! It's the *Hamlet* one.

> There's rue for you, and here's some for me.
> We may call it herb of grace o' Sundays. O, you
> must wear your rue with a difference!

Ophelia. She was crazy. It's always bugged me that Mom took my name from a crazy person's ravings, but maybe Ophelia really knew something about herbs. Maybe Shakespeare did.

The sonnet Mr. Cates read said poems are a living record of memory. Shakespeare wrote about people to make them last forever. Constance tried to use the codex to hold on to Wilkie. Words make things real. Words remember people.

I'll write each possible rue rhyme in the codex and let the words do battle against the void. My hand shakes as I carefully copy Ophelia's words. I don't want to make a mistake.

I write the last word from the passage.

Nothing happens.

I read the whole thing aloud.

Nothing.

I read the rosemary words off the back of my hand. I read the rue words and try to wrap them around the idea of Shelby.

Nothing.

My mom calls down the hallway. "Any luck?"

"Not yet," I answer, hoping she can't hear the despair in my voice.

"You want any help?"

Yes. Yes, I want help.

"No, thanks, Mom." I call back. "I should do this on my own. I love you."

"Love you too, Rosie."

The lines from *Hamlet* aren't the right words. I need to collect all the passages with rue and try them all. But what am I even trying? How do I know that reading the words aloud will do anything? Maybe I have to, I don't know, brew a potion, or turn three times and spit, or . . . Even if I find the right words, how will I know?

It's strange and sad to be doing this on my own. Adam should read the words while I write them down. Or the other way around. He should help me think of ways to test the words, to figure out which ones will work. He should wield his graph paper like a sword. But he doesn't remember, and he won't come. It's late now, anyway, nearly midnight. I have to keep looking.

I find the next *rue* on page fourteen, but it's not the right kind. It's from *Henry VI: And, in thy closet pent up, rue my shame, And ban thine enemies, both mine and thine!* This is regret, not the herb. But I write it anyway, because forgetting is our enemy, and maybe the words will ban forgetting. But they don't.

The next one, also from *Henry VI,* is the same meaning, more regret. And another one about regret from a play called *King John*. So far, *Hamlet* is the only one where the rue is a plant, but I'm not even halfway through the results.

Page twenty, and I'm almost at the midpoint, 400 out of 942. But . . . there's no "next" button to click! Where are the rest of the results? I scroll up. *Because there are so many results, only the first 20 pages will be displayed*. But I need the rest! I need all the results!

I click on Advanced Search, and there's a way to search for the exact word only. I should have checked this before, but it doesn't matter. It should get me to the right rue now.

Only sixteen hits on *rue.* Not *true* or *cruel* or *misconstrue.* Just rue.

The first seven are ones I already found. The next is from *Macbeth*. My heart breaks into a trot. That's the play that has a witch's spell in it. Mom laughed and doesn't believe it, but I know better. Adam knows better. Or he would if he remembered.

I copy the words: *You'll rue the time that clogs me with this answer.* It's regret again, but it's *Macbeth.* I have to hope. I study the words on the page. Whisper them out loud.

Nothing. Nothing. And more nothing.

Okay. Next is the same meaning from *Richard II.* All these forgotten kings . . .

Another one from the same play. Oh! Here's the plant. I copy out the whole passage:

> Poor queen! so that thy state might be no worse,
> I would my skill were subject to thy curse.
> Here did she fall a tear; here in this place
> I'll set a bank of rue, sour herb of grace:
> Rue, even for ruth, here shortly shall be seen,
> In the remembrance of a weeping queen.

Curse, remembrance. This must be it! But the words just sit dumb on the page. I read them aloud. Again.

Well, of course, Shelby wouldn't appear in my room. That wouldn't make any sense. I press my nose to the cool windowpane, completely sure I'll see Shelby outside.

The moon-colored snow sparkles. The road hasn't been plowed. Adam's footprints have long been covered over. Even my prints heading the opposite direction are softened and vanishing. The silence of the snow is a roar of emptiness and stillness and nothingness. And Shelby's not there.

I wipe away tears with the back of my hand. The black ink there smears.

Shelby. I grab on to her and snatch at hope at the same time. She won't appear on the street outside my house in the middle of the night! Why would she? She'll be at home.

I grab my phone and call Adam, but his voice mail is full.

I hesitate only a second before calling the house. It's late, but . . . I have to know.

The phone rings. I can almost hear it filling the dark house with sound, glaring in the midnight stillness.

"Hello?" Mrs. Steiner answers in a voice slurred with sleep.

Adam's dad grumbles something I can't understand in the background.

"I'm sorry to call so late," I say in a rush. "Is Shelby there?"

"Shelby?" Mrs. Steiner mumbles. "You have the wrong number."

"But . . ." I protest. "No!"

A shuffle, and then Mr. Steiner's voice, just on the edge of angry. "There is no Shelby here."

The line goes dead.

My hands are ice cold as I turn the pages of the codex back to the void poem. I clamp my lips between my teeth so I won't mouth the words. I don't look at the page straight on, like if I don't look right at it, maybe it won't be as powerful.

> Ah, treble words of absence spoken low;
> For ears of fam'ly, friend, or willful foe.
> Speak thrice to conjure nothing on the spot.
> Who harkens here will present be forgot.
> Void and nothing. Void and nothing—all strife!
> Third's the charm. To void and nothing turn life.

Even though I didn't read it aloud, panic seizes me. What if . . .

I cry out, "Mom?"

Her voice emerges, startled, from her room. "What?"

"Uh, nothing." Relief makes me dizzy, and I close my eyes. Even the millisecond of thinking I might have sent her into the void leaves me breathless and untethered from myself.

"You okay?" Concern sharpens her tone.

"Fine," I reply. "Just . . . you were so quiet, I thought you weren't here."

"I'm here."

I open my eyes and refocus on the poem. It doesn't

mention herbs or plants of any kind. It's just words, and I guess the repetition of the words. *Speak thrice.*

Void and nothing. It's terrible. It's not death. It's just not anything. Nothing. The family, friend, or foe is simply erased, as if he or she was never even born. Except it doesn't quite work because you do remember them, at least for a little while. According to Constance, there is time to undo it before the person disappears into the void. But not much time.

Thirteen

MAYBE *RICHARD II* wasn't the right play. I turn back to the computer.

The next four *rue*s on the list all mean regret. But the last one is different. It's from that play Mom mentioned, the one with the bear. *The Winter's Tale.* How appropriate.

It's the right meaning of *rue.* And it has *rosemary* too!

I copy the passage, the last one. Hope thrills through me.

> For you there's rosemary and rue; these keep
> Seeming and savour all the winter long:
> Grace and remembrance be to you both,
> And welcome to our shearing!

I read it aloud.

Nothing happens.

I read the rosemary verse and then the rue one, like I'm solving an equation. But rosemary plus rue equals nothing.

Or they don't equal Shelby. But they do bring traces of Shakespeare into my room.

I remember the sonnet from Mr. Cates's class, the one about how a poem can be a "living record" of a person. I type *Shakespeare* and *powerful rhyme* into a new search box.

Here it is.

> Not marble, nor the gilded monuments
> Of princes, shall outlive this powerful rhyme

"This powerful rhyme," I whisper the words, taste them. A powerful rhyme turned Shelby and Wilkie into nothing, but another rhyme, one more powerful, could bring them back.

I repeat the lines from *The Winter's Tale* and try to say *remembrance* with special meaning. Nothing happens. But this is it. I am completely sure. It has rosemary and rue together, and it says *remembrance be to you both*. This must be it, but why isn't anything happening?

My fingers are numb, and I'm breathing quickly. I have to hold it together. I'm the only hope now. I have to do the remembering. I'm the living record.

I go back to my father's *Riverside Shakespeare* and

find the right place in *The Winter's Tale.* Maybe getting the context will help. It's a character called Perdita. She says *For you there's rosemary and rue.* I really wish Shakespeare had more stage directions, but it seems like Perdita would hold out the herbs, clutched in her hands.

These keep seeming and savour all the winter long. Savour must mean taste or smell, like when you savor something delicious. But *seeming* . . . The plants seem like themselves even in the winter when they can't grow?

Gentle plops as snow falls from the eaves outside. The snow is already melting.

I go back to the dictionary. The first definition of *seeming* is the action or fact of appearing to be, so I was right. Shakespeare means that rosemary and rue seem to be alive even in the winter. And the plants are what lead to *grace and remembrance,* so it's like the herbs summon memory. That's exactly what we need!

But the welcome to our shearing part I don't get at all. Like shearing a sheep? I type *shearing,* and it seems to mean just cutting—like garden shears—so maybe the plants have to be cut.

Shelby disappeared on the island, in the rosemary patch. Maybe the rosemary made the poem work, so the antidote will need rosemary and rue together. Memory and regret.

We need rosemary and rue. And maybe we need to shear them.

I slap the computer closed and hurry down the hall.

"Mom?"

She's just setting her book on her night table. "What's up? Did you find what you were looking for?"

"Sort of," I say. "But I was wondering . . . I mean, it might help . . . with the project . . . if I could see some real rue. The plant, you know. Is it, uh, is it the sort of thing that grows around here?"

"I don't think so." She yawns. "It's more of a warm climate plant. In any case, it wouldn't be growing in the winter."

Desperation brings tears to my eyes, and I turn my head so she won't notice.

She reaches over to turn out the light. "I suppose you could look for a sample in the herbarium at the university."

I stare into the dark and try to keep my voice light. "Herbarium?"

"Sure." She resolves into a grainy shape as my eyes adjust. "They have clippings of hundreds of different plants. It's in Goodsell—you know, the biology building. On the top floor. You can go tomorrow, if you want."

This is too good to be true!

"Night, Rosie."

"Good night, Mom."

Following Constance's example, I leave the bathroom light off as I brush my teeth and stare into the night. The snow reflects the streetlights and the sliver of crescent moon. The limbs of the pine tree just by the window quiver, and a clump of snow drops to the ground. Already the white piles on our neighbor's lawn furniture have the rounded edges they get after a couple of days of melting. There'll still be plenty of snow for sledding in the morning, but Mom was right. It won't last more than a day.

As I wash my face, a memory rises to the surface of my mind. Sledding in the grove with Adam and . . . someone else I don't remember. The other person pushed us down the hill in a big inner tube, and we tipped over at the bottom, and snow filled my mouth, and it tasted sharp and then melted on my tongue, and I was weirdly aware of my tongue being a hot thing.

I rub my hands and face dry.

In the brightness of the overhead light in my room, I frown at my hands. I didn't get them really clean. Little tendrils of black curl over a faint gray smear, but I'm too tired to go back and scrub harder.

The phone wakes me.

"Hey, Rosie!" Adam's voice has that I-have-a-plan

quality. "Are you ready? We're going to the grove. The snow's melting fast, so we need to get out there."

"Okay." I stretch. "Who's coming?"

"Micah and Alex and Kendall. Maybe Jamie and Celia."

"Wait for me." I sit up, swing out of bed. "I can be at your house in ten minutes."

I throw on yesterday's clothes, run downstairs, and shove myself into my snow gear. Grab a banana. Shout goodbye to Mom and trot down to Adam's.

The sidewalk is already clear in patches, but there's still at least a foot of snow on the grass. At the end of the block, the river races past, high and fast.

We hurry to the university, pulling the green comet and the purple dish behind us.

"The best sleds always have names," Adam says to Micah, Jamie, and Celia as they meet us at the base of the hill.

"Of course," Micah agrees. "This is La Bala." He gestures toward his sled, a long red rocket-shaped thing.

"What's that mean?" I ask.

"Bullet," he answers. Then he's running up the hill, and the rest of us follow.

I tear down the hill on the purple dish, throwing myself to the side to avoid a big tree.

I trudge back to the top, and Adam and I go down together on La Bala.

"Woo-hoo!" he cries.

We coast almost all the way to the road.

"That was awesome!" I scramble out. "Let's go again."

We trek to the top of the hill. With the pressure of the sleds, the melting slope is super slippery.

"Treacherous!" I grin at Adam.

He smiles back. Nothing like snow for providing great adventures.

And I slip. I land on my side. A hard kernel of something slams into my hip.

Adam drops next to me. "Are you okay? Rosie?"

I roll onto my back. "I'm fine."

He helps me up. And then he half runs, half tramps to the top of the hill.

I press my hand against my hip. Something in my pocket jabbed into me. I yank off my mitten with my teeth and pull a piece of paper from my jeans. It's damp and hangs limp in my hands as I unfold it.

I frown as I read aloud, "*Rosemary, that's for remembrance. Pray, love, remember.*"

I suck in a lungful of the damp, warming air. I do remember. But I had forgotten.

"Adam!" I call after him. The snow won't let me run, and I slip again before I get to the top of the hill. Breathless and coated in clumps of snow that cling to my snow pants and my coat, I shove the paper at Adam. "Read this. Aloud."

As he reads, the color drains from his cheeks. He looks at me over the paper. He grasps my arm and whispers, "Shelby."

"Shelby." I say it in a louder voice, trying to make it sound real and normal. I have the vaguest image of a nice girl with long hair, but she wanders away from me.

"Shelby." I drag her back from the void.

"We forgot." Adam's eyes are wide. "But the rosemary rhyme makes us remember."

"And rue!" It comes back to me like a room suddenly flooded with light. The computer search. The herbarium! "Rosemary and rue bring remembrance. It's another Shakespeare spell," I say. "We need to get rosemary and rue."

Adam frowns. "What's rue?"

The rue verse tumbles out of my mouth. "Rue is another plant. My mom says it doesn't grow here, but they'll have some, like a dried sample, in the herbarium at the university." I explain, and I tug Adam toward the path. Goodsell is just over the crest of the hill.

"What's an herbarium?" he asks. He looks stunned.

"I guess it's like a library of plants."

"Hey!" Micah calls. "Where are you going?"

"Herbarium," Adam answers. He doesn't seem at

all aware that this is a totally weird place for us to be going.

"What?" Kendall shouts. "Where?"

"Nowhere," Micah answers for Adam. "Let's race! La Bala will shoot faster than any other sled!"

The whoops fade away as we head for Goodsell.

Inside, a sign directs us to the third floor.

The elevator is painfully slow.

Adam repeats, "*Rosemary, that's for remembrance.*"

"*Pray, love, remember,*" I answer.

We stand in the dim light of the elevator and remember. Shelby letting me wear her tutu from the dance recital, Shelby rowing the boat, Shelby leaning back in the V tree with her eyes closed, Shelby walking ahead of us with John.

"Remember," I repeat through clenched teeth, as snow drops from my side and disappears into the tired carpet, leaving only a faint, dark stain.

Fourteen

WE EXIT ON the third floor and follow the signs to the Christopher Jordan Herbarium. The tiny room is filled with four big metal cabinets and a blocky black table like the ones in the science lab at school. On the table are a gallon jug of something white, a glue gun, and one plant, the color of cooked spinach, dried and pressed between a piece of wax paper and a heavy white card.

"Where are all the other plants?" I whisper.

Adam gestures toward the thin, metal cabinets. Each one has double doors and a small white label on the side. The label shows a range of numbers, like call numbers but not from any system I ever learned about in library class.

"Do you think someone will come help us? Like a librarian, or an herb-rarian?" I ask.

"Someone has to come. This is not a normal classification system."

We wait awkwardly near the door. Adam studies the labels on the shelves. We're both completely at home in a library of books, but a library of plants has different rules.

"What was the rue spell again?" Adam asks.

I recite:

> For you there's rosemary and rue; these keep
> Seeming and savour all the winter long:
> Grace and remembrance be to you both,
> And welcome to our shearing!

His head is tipped to one side. "How do you know it's a spell?"

"I don't, but it seemed like it could be." I explain about my computer search.

"*Grace and remembrance be to you both*. It's a command," Adam says.

"Huh?"

"Like, *Pray, love, remember.* You know?"

"I guess it is. Maybe that's why I thought it seemed similar."

"Hello!" A breathless young man with curly brown hair pulled back in a ponytail appears behind us. "Sorry. The herbarium is quiet even during the semester, and now that it's break, I really wasn't expecting anyone."

"That's okay," I say. "I'm Rosemary Bennett. My mom's Claudia Bennett? She teaches English?"

"Sure!" Ponytail Man smiles. "How can I help you?"

"Uh, well, Adam—this is Adam—"

Adam offers a lame wave. Ponytail gives him a reassuring smile.

"Adam and I are doing a poetry project for school? For this creative writing elective that we get to take?" Why am I making everything a question? "Anyway, we're trying to write some poems about rosemary and rue. You know, they're herbs?"

"Right." He gives me an encouraging nod.

"Yeah. So, my mom suggested that maybe we could see some rue here."

Adam chimes in. "And rosemary, too."

Ponytail grins. "Your name is Rosemary, and you're doing a project on rosemary?"

"It's totally appropriate, right?" I manage a smile.

"Absolutely." He crosses over to an old-fashioned card catalog in the corner. "Only instead of rue, I'd think you'd want to write about Adam's Needle. You know, to see the plant-name connection through."

Adam perks up. "There's a plant called Adam's Needle? No way!"

Ponytail nods. "Way." His fingers walk through cards grown yellow and soft with age. "Unfortunately, we don't have it in our collection, but you could look it up online. You'll find some good photos. But rosemary and rue we do have." He mutters catalog numbers to himself, steps over to the first row of cabinets, and opens the door. Inside are about twenty shelves, really shallow, with folders lying in small stacks. He squats down and pulls a stack onto his knees. He sorts through the folders and extracts one. "Here's rue." He stands and turns to the cabinet behind him. "Rosemary should be . . ." He runs a finger along one metal shelf, another, and another, and frowns. "Huh."

He places the rue folder on the black table. "You can start with this. I'll have to check the online catalog to track down the rosemary."

"Thanks." Adam slides into a chair.

"No problem." Ponytail pauses in the doorway, on his way to wherever the online catalog is. "Don't touch the *Ruta graveolens.* It's fragile. And poisonous." And he's gone.

"What's ruta whatever-he-said?" I ask.

"The scientific name," Adam answers. "See?"

We look together at the label pasted onto the corner of the paper. It's typed by a real typewriter and says *Ruta graveolens, Potomac Riverbank, Franklin, West Virginia, June 17, 1923.*

"So it does grow near Pennsylvania," I observe.

"But probably not in December," Adam points out. "Did you know it was poisonous?"

"I don't know anything."

The plant arcs across the page. I was expecting it to have some color, but it's just brown, though a complicated brown with hints of rust and sage green mixed in.

"It's the same color as your eyes!" Adam exclaims.

"It is?" I thought my eyes were plain brown.

"Yeah." He looks at me intently.

I break away and focus on the plant. The stalk looks like a miniature tree branch. It's taped to the paper with a piece of thin white tape. The branches—six of them—are glued down, but one small branch hovers over the others. Somehow, over the years, it's escaped the page.

Some small leaves cluster near the stem, and, about three-quarters of the way up, the leaves thin out. At the top, there are what must have been flowers. The leaves, shaped like thin teardrops, angle upward. The flowers look like dry lentils with tiny hair-like tendrils.

I lean in and inhale a slightly spicy smell. Is that the rue or just old paper and glue?

Adam yanks me back. "Don't breathe it! It's poisonous!"

"It's dead—" I start.

"*It keeps savour all winter long.*"

"Okay. I won't breathe it," I promise. "But I will . . ." I glance over my shoulder for any sign of Ponytail man. Just an empty doorway. I put two fingers between the one loose branch and the paper. Before I can think twice or Adam can stop me, I use my thumb to snap it off, and I'm holding a dried sprig of rue in my hand.

Adam sucks in his breath sharply.

Quick footsteps. The squeak of a rubber sole on polished tile.

I shove the rue in my coat pocket.

"According to the records—" Ponytail bustles into the room, holding an open laptop and reading from the screen. "The rosemary specimen was reported missing four years ago. I don't know why it hasn't been replaced. It's easy enough with the rosemary patch on the island. Come spring, we'll have to take some students over there to collect a replacement, but for now, I'm afraid I can't help you with rosemary. Sorry." He looks up from the screen with an apologetic smile.

"It's okay," Adam says and stands up too quickly. His chair starts to fall, but he catches it and rights it.

"Well, thanks," I say. "It was cool to see the rue at least." Rue and rosemary. *Rosemary, that's for remembrance . . . Grace and remembrance be to you both.*

"Will it help you with your project?"

In my pocket, I carefully roll the thin stem between my fingers. "Definitely."

"Of course you could just buy rosemary at the grocery store," Ponytail says. "Though I suppose that's not very poetic."

He's right. We have rue, and we can get rosemary easily, but we still don't know what we need to do with the herbs.

We say thanks and don't talk as we walk back to the elevator. The swish of our snow pants is mortifyingly loud in the long corridor.

Adam pushes the elevator button. We wait.

Doors slide open. We step inside. Doors slide shut.

Adam looks at me like he doesn't quite know me. "I can't believe you stole from a library! They trusted us, and you just . . . I mean, they have everything all cataloged and organized, and you just took—"

"But I had to!" I protest.

The doors open. He walks ahead of me.

I can't believe it! He's putting one tiny bit of a dried plant above his sister! Somehow, even though I know I did the right thing, he's managed to make me feel guilty.

I follow him, not trying to catch up but keeping pace. By the time we're near the grove, the guilt has twisted into rage.

I lunge forward and yank him around. "I don't know what you thought we were going to get from just seeing the plant. We need to have it. The spell doesn't work without the herbs." I rip the small sprig of rue from my pocket and wave it in his face. "This is the antidote! The antidote to that horrible poisonous void poem. That we said!" I'm crying now, and Adam's pulling away from me.

"You're losing it, Rosie," he murmurs.

"It's our fault!" I sob and clutch the rue. "Shelby would know what to do, but we have to figure it out, because she's gone, and that's the problem. We need her. And she's your sister. Who we disappeared. Do you remember?"

The question arcs out over the snow and dissolves into silence. Maybe he doesn't. My anger and sadness pivot into alarm.

"Do you? Adam? Do you remember?"

"What do you mean?" Beneath his anger, I hear confusion.

I grasp him by both arms and recite the memory spell.

"I remember," he whispers. "Thanks, Rosie."

"We have rue," I say in a firm voice. "And I only took a small piece."

He nods.

"But we don't have rosemary. Like the guy said, we could buy some. Or, we could find the bookmark. Maybe we can find it? Maybe it's in your room?"

"I don't know." He rubs a hand over his face. "I had it when I left your house the other night . . ."

"You dropped it," I say. "But you picked it up."

"How do you know?"

"I saw you from the window. You put it in your pocket."

He yanks off his glove and reaches into one pocket. Then the other. He shakes his head.

I stick my hands in his pockets. They're fleecy and damp and empty.

He rubs his hand over his face again. "Okay, I must've dropped it after that."

"Let's go check your room," I say. "Maybe you took it out and put it away but then you forgot. Anyway, if we can't find it, we'll just get my mom to take us shopping."

"Or we could go to the island," Adam suggests.

We walk together down the hill. Grass already pokes up through the snow in the tracks left by our sleds.

As we cross George Street, we pause to watch the river race angry and bold to the south. Muddy water has crept over the launch, and the rowboat strains as the current tugs it downstream.

"Do you think we can even get to the island?" I ask. "I mean, if we want to go."

The water is dark, like it's churning stuff up from the bottom, and it's running so fast that things—branches and hunks of ice—race along with the current.

Adam doesn't answer. Rowing through that water is out of the question.

We squish through the soggy snow in Adam's backyard and pull off our boots in the mudroom. We enter the kitchen in our socks.

Mrs. Steiner looks up from the stove. "Lunch is almost ready. Soup. Chicken with white beans."

It smells like comfort and warmth.

"Thanks, Mom." Adam heads for the stairs. "We just need to look for something first."

Adam's room is ridiculously tidy. Everything has a place, and everything is in its place. Square plastic bins with neatly printed labels line the shelf in the closet. The drawers are filled with carefully folded clothes. Nothing is under the bed. No dirty clothes or half-read books clutter the floor. I can tell instantly that the rosemary bookmark is not here.

Mrs. Steiner's voice wafts up the stairs. "Lunch! Come eat!"

We sit at the table, and Mrs. Steiner puts supersized bowls of soup in front of us. She's a really good cook, but since she started working so much, she hasn't had much time to spend in the kitchen. Shelby cooked sometimes, but then she got too busy, too. And now she's gone.

Adam blows on a spoonful of golden broth.

I lean in to inhale the steam rising from my bowl. Along with the rich smell of chicken, there's a familiar piney smell.

"Mrs. Steiner, does this have rosemary?" I ask.

Adam looks up at his mother.

"Yes," she says, ladling out a bowl for herself. "I love rosemary with white beans."

"Do we have any more?" Adam asks.

"You think it needs more?" She frowns and tastes the soup.

"No," I say. "The soup is perfect. But we're still working on that poetry project. You know? For Mr. Cates? And we thought it would be . . . well, it's hard to explain, but we need some rosemary."

She crosses to the fridge and rummages in a small drawer. "I might have used it all. Let's see. Here's thyme . . . this is cilantro . . ." She pulls up a slim plastic package and wrinkles her nose. "This *was* mint. More thyme. I'll have to do something with that . . . Here's rosemary!"

Adam looks at me over his bowl.

Mrs. Steiner hands me the package. Two slight sprigs lie inside.

"It's too bad you can't go over to the island and pick your own. That would surely be more poetic than scrounging in the fridge." She sits at the table. Picks up some papers.

The table is against the wall in a windowed nook. There are only three places to sit. One for Adam. One for his dad. And one for his mom. I sit in Mr. Steiner's spot.

I pat the pocket of my jeans, feeling the outline of the folded paper. I say the rosemary verse into my bowl and picture Shelby at the table with us, but there's no space for her here.

Adam and I eat in silence. He tries to use his spoon to separate the ingredients—beans clustered in one area, carrots nearby, and chicken on the other side of the bowl.

"It's soup, dork," I say through a full mouth. "All the stuff is supposed to be mixed up. Same's true for salad, actually."

He grins at me sheepishly. "I can't help it. You know how I like to do separate bites and together bites." He makes careful and strategic maneuvers with his spoon.

"But it all floats back together." I try not to laugh.

"I just have to be persistent."

My phone rings.

I tug it from my pocket. "It's my mom."

"Rosie?" I can hear the worry in her voice.

"What's wrong?"

Adam and Mrs. Steiner both look at me.

"Well." She's perplexed, not worried. "This is rather odd. I just got a call from a nurse at River House . . ."

"Is Constance okay?" I look at Adam.

His jaw clenches.

I bite the inside of my cheek.

"I'm not exactly sure," she answers. "The nurse said she's been unusually agitated and she keeps asking for you." She finishes on a note of surprise.

"For me?"

Adam's forehead crinkles into a question. "For you what?"

"Evidently." Mom sighs. "She says, 'Rosemary. I need Rosemary.' Over and over again. The nurse says she's never been like this before, and she wondered if you might be able to come see her. It all seems strange to me, but . . . she's an old woman with no family . . . Would you mind? I'll come pick you up. I don't think we'll need to stay there for long."

"Of course. I don't mind."

She sighs with relief. "I'll be there in a few minutes."

"Can Adam come too?" I ask.

He gives me a thumbs-up.

"I don't see why not," she says.

"It's awfully nice of you two to take an interest in Constance Brooke," Mrs. Steiner says.

"She doesn't have anyone," I reply simply, but it's not simple. My eyes dart to the fourth side of the Steiners' table, the side pushed against the wall. The side for no one.

Fifteen

MOM INSISTED ON STAYING with us. She, Adam, and I sit jammed in a semicircle of chairs too close to Constance's bed. A nurse lurks in the doorway.

Constance's face is blank. She doesn't recognize me or Adam.

"Do I know you?"

"I'm Rosemary," I remind her.

"Oh, rosemary!" She nods, but her face remains still. "Father is just wonderful with rosemary, you know. He always says . . ." Her voice trails off.

"Constance," the nurse urges her. "You asked for Rosemary. Do you remember?"

"Remember," Constance echoes.

I reach for Constance's hand. It's so light, I'm afraid I will hurt her just by touching her.

She closes her fingers around mine and looks into

my face. She whispers, "There's something I've forgotten." Her eyelids droop, then close. Her mouth drops open slightly.

"She's asleep," I whisper.

"Should we leave?" Adam asks.

She summoned us. This has to be important. "Let's wait."

Mom's face is pinched. "Such a horrid disease," she murmurs. She looks away, her jaw clenched, and rummages in her bag. "I should've brought a book." She pulls out a folded newspaper and starts to read.

I wish I could disappear into reading too, but I owe Constance my attention. I watch her chest rise and fall. It shudders with each breath as her body labors to do its job, the job of keeping her alive.

Adam taps my arm, jarring me away from my morbid thoughts. "What?" I snap.

He thrusts his jaw at Mom's newspaper. At the brightly colored weather map on the back page. A big yellow blob that looks like a quotation mark, half dot and half curvy arrow, sits over Pennsylvania. In the middle of the blob it says "mild" in a friendly font. In the corner, just by Florida, a chart shows the phases of the moon. Tomorrow night is the new moon.

All warmth and patience drain out of me. I press Constance's hand. She has to wake up.

She stirs. Her eyelids are still heavy, and she doesn't seem aware that anyone is here.

I lean in and whisper in her ear. "Tomorrow is the new moon."

She blinks and focuses on me.

"All is lost," she murmurs.

"What's that?" Mom sets the paper on her lap.

"It's from her poem," Adam says quickly. "'Moon Mangled Memory.'"

Constance sits up taller and speaks firmly. "I want to talk to the girl and boy. Alone."

Mom turns to look at the nurse. "I don't know . . ."

"It's fine." The nurse holds the door open. "She's calm now."

"Rosie—" Mom begins.

"We'll be fine," I assure her.

Mom hesitates, then follows the nurse into the hallway. The door clicks shut.

Constance searches my face and Adam's. "I don't know you. Can you help me?"

I recite the rosemary verse.

Her hand spasms in mine. Her eyes shift out of focus. "Wilkie. Wilkie."

"Constance"—I lean in again—"the new moon is tomorrow night. We have the rhyme and rue and rosemary. What do we need to do? Please. You have to remember."

"I ran out of time." Her voice is small, constricted by grief.

"I know." I choke back a sob. "But we still have time. Please help us."

Her throat spasms. Her eyes dart from side to side as if watching the memory play out in her mind. "I had to get home. For . . . for . . ."

"Rosemary?" I prompt.

"Wilkie!" Her face screws up in silent anguish. She makes no sound, but loss contorts her expression.

There is nothing we can do for her. I sit with her hand in my lap, my body heavy and awkward with its uselessness. Adam hovers behind me.

Finally, she closes her mouth. She looks from me to Adam. "Hello. Do I know you?"

The blankness on her face is a heartbreaking relief. Sometimes forgetting is better. Mom was right.

And I don't want to tell her my name, because rosemary might make her remember, and the loss will burst over her again.

Adam whispers, "Wilkie is lost, but Shelby isn't. We have to go."

I turn to tell Constance we're leaving, but she grabs my wrist, and now her grip is strong, each one of the bones in her hand pressing into my flesh.

She speaks slowly and clearly:

Ah, treble words of absence spoken low;
For ears of fam'ly, friend, or willful foe.
Speak thrice to conjure nothing on the spot.

"No!" Adam and I gasp at once.

She doesn't hear us.

Who harkens here—

"Stop!" I twist out of her grip. "Constance, you have to stop!"

I grasp her shoulders and shake her once, trying to make her look at me, but her gaze just slides away.

—will present be forgot

Adam tugs on my arm. "We have to get away. If we don't hear it, it won't . . . it can't . . ." He drags me to the door. "Rosie, c'mon!"

Void and nothing. Void and nothing—all strife!

"Please stop!" I sob.

Adam fumbles with the door knob.

Third's the charm.

"Rosemary!" Adam grabs me around the waist and lifts me to the doorway.

"Rosemary?" Constance's voice lilts upward. She sees us. Smiles. "Why, hello. Do I know you?"

Adam sets me down but keeps hold of me, and I cling to his arm across my middle.

My legs tingle, and my heart races.

"I'm Rosemary," I choke out. "And this is Adam."

Adam releases me, and I drop into the chair. He crosses to the bed.

"What were you thinking?" He asks, sounding wounded.

Constance studies him. Closes her eyes for a moment. "What were you thinking?" she echoes. "Father asked the same question. He pulled me from the water. So cold. What were you thinking?" She opens her eyes. She looks sad and worried and bewildered. "What was I thinking? Do you know?"

Remembering will hurt her, but I recite the spell. She needs to know, and she'll forget again.

"Rosemary is for remembrance," she echoes, her voice tight. "And rue is for regret. Yes. I remember. Father might have made it to the island, even in the flood. He might have made it in time. But he had to save me. He chose me. *He chose me.* And then there was only me."

I clap my hand to my mouth. Wilkie might have been saved, and Constance . . .

She looks at me dully, waiting for the relief of forgetting to kick in.

This is too cruel. I stand quickly, and my chair squeals against the floor.

The door opens. Mom sticks her head in. "Everything all right?" she asks.

"Fine," I lie.

"And how are you?" Constance gazes at us, her head cocked slightly to one side, like a bird's. Her voice is light, her face relaxed.

"Fine," Adam answers.

"Would you care for a peppermint?" She raises a skeletal arm to the candy dish on the table. Offers a gentle and empty smile.

"No, thank you," I reply. Already, Wilkie is gone.

In the car, Mom peppers us with questions about our conversation with Constance. We give her vague half-truths.

She sighs. "Dementia is a dreadful thing. So much worse than a physical disability."

"It must be awful at the beginning." I look out the window at the rising water. "When you're with it enough to realize that you're losing it."

The car lurches to a stop.

"Sorry," Mom mutters. "River Road is closed."

Yellow lights flash on either side of a big sign. ROAD CLOSED. FLOODING.

I bite the inside of my cheek. Look at Adam.

Mom swings the car around in a tight U-turn and takes the long way home.

She chatters about some kind of cookie she wants to make, and Adam and I take turns making interested noises, but we're both preoccupied. I keep hearing Constance's steady voice. *Void and nothing. Third's the charm.*

I try to drown her out with the rosemary verse. I whisper it, and Adam joins in.

I reach into my pocket and rub my fingertip along the rue stem. We have rue. We have rosemary. We have the poem. It's not yet the new moon. It's going to be okay. In my mind, Shelby's laugh sounds and drifts away.

Adam and I sit cross-legged on my bed, the codex open between us. The stolen rue, golden brown and dried, lies across Mrs. Steiner's rosemary, which looks like a tiny branch from a Christmas tree. The herbs make an X across the page.

"Ready?" I ask.

He reaches for my hand but recoils. "What's that?"

I follow his stare down to angry red blisters on my fingers. "Ew." The rash is on the pads of my index and middle finger and also on my thumb.

"The rue," I say. "I was touching it in my pocket."

Adam raises his eyebrows. "I guess it's still poisonous, even though it's dead."

"It keeps savour all winter long." I extend my other hand. "That means it should work."

We hold hands across the book, because it seems like what you should do when you're performing a magic spell. I don't mean to, but I squeeze Adam's hand. He squeezes back.

I look down at the open page. My writing looks back at me. *For you there's rosemary and rue.* Shakespeare wrote those words, and then I did. And I wonder what happened in the four hundred years in between. How many people needed these words? Needed this magic? Needed to rescue someone from the void?

Adam's voice catches as he begins, and I hold his hand tightly. I match the pace of my reading to his. Our voices in unison sound like church.

> For you there's rosemary and rue; these keep
> Seeming and savour all the winter long:
> Grace and remembrance be to you both,
> And welcome to our shearing!

My tongue sticks on the thickness of the *th* sound at the end of *both*. And then the silence in my room presses on me.

Nothing happens.

We wait, Adam gripping my fingers until they hurt.

Still nothing.

I can't meet his eyes. It didn't work. Because the rosemary was from the store, and we didn't shear it, or because the rue is too dry, or because the time is wrong, or because the place is wrong. Or because magic isn't real.

"Do you think we need to hold the herbs?" Adam asks.

The hope in his voice makes me wince.

I let myself sink into memories of Shelby. I let them wash over me like waves, and they sting against the rawness of my heart because I know I'll soon forget. This is how Constance must have felt when she first learned she had Alzheimer's.

Shelby and I lean against the branches of the V tree and talk about how we want to travel when we grow up. When we get back to her house, we open a map of Europe and plot our journey.

Shelby helps me and Adam pick our classes for eighth grade. Her whole face lights up when she talks about Mr. Cates.

Shelby gives me a bag of clothes she's outgrown.

Shelby and I sit on her bed, a pile of books between us. She explains a little bit about each one, little blurbs specially crafted for me, because she knows what I like.

Shelby can't come with me and Adam to the library because she's hanging out with Maria and Pam. She can't come play Scrabble because she's going out with John.

Shelby can't come help set up my room . . . but then she does. She carries my books, and it's like she drags bound bits of me down the hall.

Tomorrow it will be too late. Shelby will be gone. Into the void. And unless we remember to remember, we won't even know we've lost her.

Tears well up and tumble down my cheeks.

Adam looks down at the plants and the book. "We have the rosemary and the rue and the rhyme."

"This powerful rhyme," I murmur.

"What's missing is the place." He looks up. "We have to go to the island."

"We can't." I look out the window. Mean hunks of ice and clublike branches course past, carried by the racing, muddy water.

Adam watches the river too. "It's like algebra," he says in a low voice. "We have solved three of the variables. We have to plug in the fourth one."

"X equals the island?"

"It has to, doesn't it?" he says.

The river's like a stampede, rushing forward, trampling over everything in its path. It's too dangerous—my brain and the animal instinct part of me both know this—but if Shelby were in the water, being carried along with all the debris, waving, sputtering, drowning, we wouldn't just watch. We would do something.

"Okay," I say softly.

Adam's eyes are wet with tears, and his throat spasms as he swallows hard. "Thank you."

He scrambles off the bed, dragging the codex after him, along with the afghan wrapped around his ankle. It thuds to the floor. He untangles himself and stumbles to the door.

"I'll be back," he grumbles.

He disappears down the hall. I hear the water running in the bathroom.

I watch the river. Something blocky races by, a piece of wood or metal, carried by the current. Hunks of ice hurtle downstream.

Adam returns. He sits next to me on the bed. We watch the river in silence, our knees pressed together. Another manmade thing hurries past.

"Was that a cooler?" Adam asks.

"Maybe."

A memory breaks over me. Adam and me in a kiddie pool in his backyard. Someone spraying us with a hose. His dad? It must have been. And us laughing and laughing and laughing. And then lying on our backs looking up through the branches of the big pine tree in his yard. Just breathing.

But some part of the memory escapes me. Me and Adam and Mr. Steiner? That's not quite right. Absently, I rub the rash on my fingers. They feel hot and swollen.

Something pokes my hip. A wadded paper in my pocket. I fish it out and toss it into the wastebasket.

"Two points!" Adam sings out, but his voice makes me flinch. His easy tone jars me. I don't know why.

Sixteen

WE WATCH VIDEOS online until Adam has to go home. He gets up to leave and trips over a book on the floor. He bends to pick up the old diary we found in the cupboard.

He holds it loosely in one hand.

The pages arch around something stuck inside.

I reach for the book.

The angry welts on my fingers make my hand look like it's not mine. I watch this stranger's hand, swollen and red, take the old diary with its cracked burgundy binding that feels like skin.

The book opens eagerly. Two plants—one dry and brown, the other moist and green—wait on the page.

"Rosemary," I murmur.

Adam stares at me, but he's looking at something, someone who isn't here. *Rosemary, that's for remembrance. Pray, love, remember.*

"Shelby!" I cry.

Adam's jaw is set, his face grim. "We have to go now. Tomorrow is the new moon, and if we forget again . . ."

I finish. "It will be too late."

Adam takes the plants and clutches them tight.

"The rue," I caution. "You'll get a rash."

"I don't care. I have to hold on. I have to remember."

I don't point out that the rash didn't help me remember.

"Let's go," he says, moving quickly toward the door.

"Wait," I say. He stops. "It's suicide to go in the dark. We can't save Shelby if we kill ourselves. You saw all that debris. We'll get knocked over. We'll drown."

"But if we wait until morning, we might forget." Adam's eyes fill with tears. "We will forget. And Shelby will be gone. Forever. And we won't even know."

"Constance almost died trying to save Wilkie," I remind him. "And her father had to rescue her. He probably nearly died, too. We can't let the poem take all three of us. We just have to remember," I say with a firmness I don't feel. "We'll write the rosemary line everywhere."

I take a thick black pen from my desk and hand Adam a blue marker. I write on the back of his left hand and the palm of his right. *Rosemary, that's for remembrance.*

I hold out my hands, and he writes on me. *Pray, love, remember.* He murmurs the words over and over as he writes them.

We both lean over the desk, writing the lines on scraps of paper. We fill our pockets with the words.

I copy the lines onto a stack of sticky notes and put them around my room. On each window and each dresser drawer. On the green cushion of my chair. On the closet door, and my headboard, and a whole bunch all over the desk. I stick them on my bookshelves next to the labels Adam made—*Pray, love, remember* ROSIE'S SPECIAL BOOKS. I place the last note on the cupboard door.

Adam stands at the front door, his temporarily tattooed hands limp at his sides.

I hug him and say into a mouthful of his hair, "We will remember. The words won't let us forget."

I feel him swallow, his throat pressed against the side of my face.

"We'll meet at the launch first thing in the morning," I say.

He pulls back and walks away from me. I watch him go, but I hold him in my mind. He stands there with Shelby, both of them solid and sure, and when the edges of Shelby go blurry, I hiss, "*Rosemary, that's for remembrance,*" and hold forgetting at bay.

I chase dreams all night, or they chase me. When I wake up, a hot metal taste fills my mouth. I run my tongue over the raw inside of my cheek.

I rub the exhaustion out of my eyes and stare at the thick blue writing on my palm. The *y*'s have little loops on their tails, like Adam's *y*'s always do. Something about seeing his writing on my skin grounds me and holds me together.

Outside, the snow is gone. All except those icy, gray mounds that won't melt until spring. And the river still runs dangerously fast. Going to the island is a bad idea. A really, really bad idea. But it's the only idea.

I hurry into leggings and a long shirt. Somewhere in the back of my mind is a warning about how heavy jeans get when they're wet and the grim certainty that I'm going into the river today.

I tell Mom I'm going to Adam's. He'll tell his parents he's coming over here. Before anyone realizes, we'll already be on the island.

I jog down the road to the boat launch, or what is usually the boat launch but is now overflowed river, creeping all the way up to the road. Another one of those big signs with lights blinks nearby. ROAD CLOSED. FLOODING.

Adam rounds the corner with glaring orange life vests hanging over his arm. Life preservers meant to preserve life. I teeter between panic that we need them and relief that he brought them.

We don't speak. There's nothing to say.

The boat is still tied to its post, but the rope is taut, and the boat strains downstream like a dog pulling on its leash. We step into the murk to wade over to the boat. The water slices into my skin, so cold that it burns. My lungs tighten, and my blood races, trying to keep me warm, trying to warn me. Screaming at me to get my body out of danger.

"Adam, I . . ." But my protest dies before I shape it into words. We are Shelby's life preservers.

My legs are numb. I smack my thighs to get the blood flowing, and pins and needles shoot down toward my knees. My lungs are still tight, even though I don't feel the cold now.

I force myself to Adam's side.

He grabs the edge of the boat. "Here." He puts a life vest over my head.

My hands shake as I struggle to tie the long nylon strap around my waist.

Adam reaches over and finishes the knot for me.

"Why aren't you shaking?" I mutter.

He doesn't answer. He reaches for a handle on the side of the boat. A series of memories hurries through my mind, like flipping pages in a book. Adam pulling the boat toward Shelby. Shelby holding the boat steady while I climb in. Me holding the boat, Shelby reaching over me, helping me. "I've got it," she says, smiling.

A snap. The boat lurches away again.

Adam stares at the broken handle in his hand. It's dirty off-white plastic, with screws jagging from its back where the boat should be. "It broke off," he says.

"I see that." I swallow hard.

Adam drops the useless piece of plastic into the frigid water. I expect it to bob there in the strange currents of this flooded part of the river, the part that isn't supposed to be here, but it sinks, and it's gone.

Adam lurches to the boat. His hands are shaking now. From cold? From fear?

I tell my legs to move. One step. Another. My brain struggles with the weird sensation of being in the river and feeling the street under my feet.

I stand with Adam, the boat rope tight against our thighs.

"We have to pull it in," he says. "Together. The river's stronger than me."

We alternate hands on the rope, like we're setting up for tug of war, and we pull. I use my legs and my back and all the strength I can find in my arms. The boat reluctantly inches toward us.

Together, we grasp the side. It tips, and the oars tumble against the wooden slats, making a horrible clatter.

"Pull!" Adam grunts.

We yank the boat toward us, out of the racing current. As soon as there's enough slack in the rope, I struggle to unloop it from the post. My hands are numb now too, and my fingers are thick and clumsy. It takes me four tries to untie the boat.

I watch my hands, like they are something apart from me. The ink has washed away, leaving only a faint tinge of blue and no words. Anything in my pocket will be soaked and ruined. The words are all washing away, but I keep Shelby in my head. I say her name over and over as I fight with the rope, turning it into two syllables that are like breathing. *Shel-by. Shel-by. Shel-by.*

"Shel-by," I whisper. "Shel-by."

Adam recites, "*Rosemary, that's for remembrance. Pray, love—*"

"I remember," I cut in. Shelby is usually the one who does the rope when we take the boat to the island. My hands fighting with the current and the rope and the cold wetness are like her hands. She's not gone. She's in my head. In my memory. Until tonight when no moon will rise. *Absent souvenir. All is lost.*

The rope comes loose, and I twine it quickly around my wrist. The boat wants to dart away, and the rope burns my skin as it resists.

Adam's face is red from working so hard to hold the boat. "Get in," he growls through clenched teeth.

I hoist myself into the boat. A million pins and needles stab into me as my legs leave the water. I turn away from the pain. Grab an oar and do my best to work against the current. I trust to instinct and to the strength that comes out of nowhere in a crisis to brace the flat of the oar against the racing water and hold the boat steady.

Adam clambers into the boat, and for just a heartbeat, I hold us still, but I'm not strong enough. We lurch downstream.

The boat crashes into a tree stump on what's normally the bank, and waits there for a second. Then we shoot out into the main part of the river.

Adam and I battle the water with our oars. My arm muscles are working at full strength but accomplishing nothing. I've always felt so in control when we row over to the island. We're independent and knowledgeable about the river and the boat and ourselves. But now . . . All that slips away, racing downstream with the branches and hunks of plastic.

Something huge hurtles our way.

"What is that?" I shout.

"Car door," Adam answers, his eyes wide.

Bright, angry red and dull gray, the door speeds

toward us. We fight against the current, but it holds us fast. I numbly pull in my oars. Adam follows my lead. We curl into each other, waiting for impact and then for the icy water. I try to think of a plan, but my mind is stalled. I wrap my arms around Adam's forearm, looped around my waist, over the bottom of my life vest, and I hope, hope, hope that the vest will do its job. That it will preserve me. That I will stay afloat. And not hit my head or get pulled under or . . .

The heavy piece of metal and plastic slams into the back of the boat, and everything stops. We're not moving. The door and the boat crash together and somehow make stillness. Then we pitch, not forward, but sideways. We're closer to the island. And out of the current.

The door dances past, like a leaf in the raging water.

"Quick!" Adam grasps his oars.

I snatch mine. Even as the boat careens downstream, we're able to propel ourselves across. We move steadily at an angle. Down and over. More down than over, and I worry we'll overshoot the island. If that happens . . . I don't know the southern part of the river well. There isn't another island for a long ways. If we don't make it to our island, we'll just have to ride the current. If we can.

I've never worked so hard in my life. My arms are

on fire, and I'm sure I've torn a muscle, but we keep plunging in the oars and shoving through the water.

We're close now. If the river weren't so crazy, we could swim for it from here. We're almost there, but we're still moving down way faster than we're moving over. In a few minutes we'll be past the island. It will be too late.

"Throw the rope!" I shout.

A huge branch knocks into us, and I pitch forward. My face slams into the side of the boat. Tears burst into my eyes.

"You okay?"

I wipe blood from my nose.

Adam stands in the boat. I work the oars. He makes a lasso and looks for a target. The boat rocks and bobs, but Adam is still. He raises his arm, lets out his breath, and tosses the rope. It sails over the churning river and catches on the broken branch of a fallen tree, sticking up like a thumb just at the edge of the island.

The boat lurches as the loop catches, and Adam falls to his knees, but the rope holds.

Seventeen

ADAM CINCHES UP his life vest and jumps into the water. It comes just above his knees, and he wades quickly to the shore.

My face is throbbing, and a rivulet of blood runs down my vest. I have to get out of the boat. I follow Adam. The cold water burns again. My lungs tighten. I stumble against something under the water and fall.

I thrust my arms forward to catch myself.

Pain.

Pain like nothing I've felt before. Ever.

Shooting up and down my arm.

It won't move.

I can't move it.

My life vest holds my head out of the water, but I'm too dizzy to stand up.

I am nothing but pain.

"Rosie?"

I try to take a deep breath, but even that small

movement stabs my arm. I gulp a mouthful of silty water. Spit. Close my eyes against the flashes that must be what people mean when they talk about seeing stars.

I just hang in the river, suspended by the orange vest, my left hand clinging to the rope, my right arm dangling useless. The pain spikes out from my elbow. The cold water is numbing, but every time the river pulls at my arm, a wave of nausea engulfs me.

"I'm coming." Adam pulls himself along the rope, back toward me.

I wonder dimly how he could possibly help.

He grabs hold of my vest and pulls me onto my feet. He reaches for my arm and then looks away. Swallows hard.

"I think . . . I'm pretty sure you dislocated your elbow," he says, not looking.

"Okay," I agree. Yes, that sounds right. Except *dislocated* is too dull a word for how this feels. Swearwords that I've never spoken, that I didn't even know I knew, rise up inside me, but I keep my mouth shut. If I open my mouth, I'll throw up.

And then I do anyway. The vomit hurries away with the current. Just more debris racing downstream.

Adam puts an arm around my waist and guides me through the shallow water to the bank. "You have to step up here." He half lifts me onto a log.

I'm on dry land. Shaking. Shuddering. And with every tremor my arm throbs.

Adam undoes his life vest and lifts up the tail of his shirt. He blots at my face. Gently touches the bridge of my nose.

"It doesn't look broken," he says. "Just bloody."

"Okay," I say. I would cut off my nose if it would stop the pain in my arm.

"Your arm . . ." Adam is at a loss. "Can you . . . ? We have to get to the Rosie patch. Rosemary? Do you hear me? We'll go to the patch and do the poem and get Shelby back, and then we'll get you to a hospital. Okay? Rosie?"

I fight through the crowding cobwebs in my head. Adam looks scared. He said we would get Shelby back. Who's Shelby?

"Shelby?" I ask, but my teeth are chattering, so it comes out a quavering *She-el-by?*

Adam grasps my shoulders.

Pain. I sway.

He holds me steady and recites firmly, "*Rosemary, that's for remembrance. Pray, love, remember.*"

Shelby sits across from me, leaning against a tree branch, high up. Her hair blows slightly in the breeze. She reads aloud from *Pelagia's Boats.* My favorite book. A book Shelby gave me. About hope and starting over.

I remember.

Adam fumbles at his waist. Undoes his belt.

I use all my energy to stay on my feet and to not throw up again.

He wraps the belt across my shoulder and down. "Rosie, I'm going to lift your arm into this. Like a sling, okay?"

"Will it feel better?" I so want it to feel better.

"I think . . . I think it will help it not feel worse," he says.

I take a deep breath and . . .

The scream rips from me like pain in the shape of sound.

"I'm sorry. I'm sorry. I'm sorry." Adam settles my wrist against his belt.

Waves of pain and sickness break over me. And again. And again.

And then I'm okay, or not okay, but better.

I meet Adam's worried gaze and whimper, "Let's go."

"I'm sorry," he whispers.

"Let's go," I repeat. "While I can."

We walk along the path through underbrush and over small puddles of snow that lie in the shade of trees. I have to focus on breathing and stepping and holding Shelby in my memory so I know why I'm not just curling up and waiting for rescue.

I *am* the rescue.

We are.

Step. Breathe. Step. Breathe.

The rosemary patch is in front of us. We climb the small hill. Adam pushes through the thick bushes and holds some branches back so I can pass.

The scent surrounds us. Piney and sharp. And thoughts of Shelby fill me. She hands me her copy of a book. She smiles and says, "You'll take good care of it." She twirls to that fast Russian dance song from *The Nutcracker.* I ask, "Can you show me how to do that?" And she does. She tells me that she likes a boy, and she has a big, silly, embarrassed grin on her face, and then I do, too, when she tells me I'm the only one who knows.

Adam brushes against my bad arm. An ache stabs all through me. I make a sharp animal sound.

"Sorry!" He puts a hand on my other arm, gentle and warm.

We stand in the little clearing where we sat with Shelby when we read the void poem. The Barbie lies there, pressed into the earth. A small leaf has fallen on her lap, and she looks like a messed-up Eve from the Garden of Eden. I want to point this out to Adam —Adam and Eve—but the signal from my brain can't get past my elbow, and I can't point.

We're where we need to be. We have the herbs. It's not yet the new moon. All we have to do is say the poem. I think. I hope.

"Let's do the poem." The words come out funny because I'm biting my cheek.

Adam pulls the rue, now soaked, from his pocket. He breaks off a fresh branch of rosemary from the plant behind me.

I close my left hand over his and over the herbs. "Ready?" I ask.

> For you there's rosemary and rue; these keep
> Seeming and savour all the winter long:
> Grace and remembrance be to you both,
> And welcome to our shearing!

Adam and I stand in the clearing, soaking wet. Pain clouds around my elbow and all down and up my arm and into my head. The Barbie lies on her side with her frozen smile.

Adam's face crumples. "It didn't work."

I cling to Shelby with my mind. "Turn your body but keep your head still as long as you can. One. Two. Three," she says as I twirl. "Good!" I'm getting it now. "Again," she says. "One. Two . . ."

"Three!" I cry out loud.

Adam holds his face in his hands.

"Three," I say again. "Three times. There was all that thrice stuff in the void poem. You know, like third time's the charm. Maybe it really is. A charm."

Adam looks up. His nose is red. Tears trail down both cheeks. "A charm?"

"Maybe we have to say the poem three times." With my good arm, I reach out for his hand again.

"Okay." His voice is small.

We try again. I don't listen to our voices chanting Shakespeare's words. I let the pine smell of the rosemary and a sort of rotten coconut smell that must be the rue fill my mouth. I let the savour of the plants sink like steam into my lungs, and I release it with the words into the rosemary patch, the Rosie patch.

And a third time.

> For you there's rosemary and rue; these keep
> Seeming and savour all the winter long:
> Grace and remembrance be to you both,
> And welcome to our shearing!

The roar of the river racing all around the island is the sound of the pain coursing through my body. A crow caws not far away. Somewhere, maybe in town, a siren, a high-pitched wail. Are they coming for us? I don't think I can make it back otherwise.

I stagger into the darkness rising around me.

And a hand steadies me. Grasps my good arm. Holds me firm and close.

It's Shelby.

Eighteen

SHELBY FROWNS at our life vests. She pushes her hair behind her ear. "What . . . ?"

But she can't ask her question because Adam collapses against her. He's sobbing. And I am, too. Relief vibrates in my skin, weaving over and under the pain.

"You guys are really freaking me out! What the heck is going on?" She stares at Adam, then at me. "Why are you all wet? Where'd the life vests come from? When did it get so cold?" She wraps her arms around Adam's quaking back and holds him. "What's the matter?"

"You—" Adam gasps. "Gone."

"What do you mean? I'm right here."

"Yes!" I cry. "But you weren't before. You've been gone for six days."

"What are you talking about? We came over because it's such a nice day, or it was." She frowns. She takes in my belt-sling. "What . . . ?"

"No time has passed for her." I get it right away. I get it because of *A Wrinkle in Time,* where they explain that maybe time can wrinkle. The book has a picture of a string, and someone folds the string, and an ant walks right across the fold. He goes from one end of the string to the other without walking on the middle because it hangs down in a loop, or a wrinkle. "There's an ant on a string," I explain.

Adam looks at me like I'm crazy, and I am. Crazy with pain, but now we have time because we have Shelby and everything will be okay. I speak slowly. "You know, our lives move on a straight line, but for Shelby, the line wrinkled, and she passed over all the days we spent forgetting her and remembering her. For Shelby, the void poem wrinkled time, and I guess if we hadn't gotten here before the new moon with the antidote poem and the rosemary and the rue, her line —her whole self—would have disappeared. Into void and nothing."

But that didn't happen. We got here in time. We found the poem. Everything is okay. Except my elbow, which, like Shelby, is out of joint. But it can be put back, too, and we won't need any magic words.

"What are you talking about?" Shelby demands.

Adam hurries through a rough explanation of what happened while we walk back to the boat. I don't help. I focus on my arm and on walking and breathing.

She says, "Shakespeare wrote magic spells?" She doesn't believe him. Why would she?

He starts pointing out changes as evidence that time has passed. It's cold. It's wet. There's snow on the ground. We're soaked. And wearing different clothes. And wearing life vests. And my elbow. "Rosie's elbow's dislocated!"

"Dislocated," Shelby echoes as we reach the bank.

The boat tugs against its rope. The river still rages.

Shelby's eyes widen as she watches a lawn chair race past, tumbling in the water.

"This is your proof," she says. Her voice goes higher. "I would never have come here with the river like this. I would never have let you come."

"We made it over," Adam assures her with a confidence I'm certain he doesn't feel. "We'll make it back. Plus, now we have you to help."

Her face is pinched with worry. "But maybe we should wait. The river will settle down. Or someone will come for us."

"She's right," I say. "If we sit here, on the bank, maybe someone in Cookfield will spot us."

"Those life vests would be hard to miss," Shelby agrees. She pulls her phone from her pocket. "No reception," she murmurs.

Adam drops onto a log. It's soaked, but so is he.

I sit beside him and prop my foot up on a stone so

that my knee can support my forearm. My arm is actually throbbing. In cartoons, exclamation points and asterisks radiate out from a bright red injury. It turns out that's a pretty realistic way to draw pain. I close my eyes and allow my head to drop onto Shelby's shoulder.

"Start at the beginning," she says.

We tell her about the codex and the void poem and Constance, putting all the pieces together for her.

Adam explains, "She lost her brother, Wilkie, here on the island, and she found the poem and figured out about the rosemary and the rue, but she didn't make it in time. It was the '24 flood, just like now, and she tried to go by herself, but she couldn't make it, and her dad had to rescue her, and then he couldn't get to the island either, and the new moon came, and it was too late."

No one says anything. The river sounds like an engine. The crow caws.

"But when a person, like, goes into the void, they're gone. Completely. Right?" Shelby asks.

Adam nods.

"But . . . you just told me about Willie." Shelby speaks slowly, trying to make this piece fit.

"Wilkie," I correct. Pain burns up my arm. Why does it hurt to talk? I bite my cheek and focus on the metallic taste of blood.

"Yeah, Wilkie," Shelby says. "You know his name. You know about him. So he's not in a void, right?"

"The rosemary line from *Hamlet* makes you remember," Adam explains. "It brings people back from the void—not really, but as memories."

Adam and I say the verse together. For Wilkie. My voice is thin with pain, but his is steady and sure.

And even though Shelby sits by my side, the line still summons memories. Only now they come slow and easy. Adam and Shelby and me on the island. So many times before and also now.

We sit in silence, remembering.

Shelby shifts slightly on the log, and I shift with her. On my other side, Adam presses in to me. They hold me up. Darkness fills my head and pushes behind my eyes. Adam's arm solid against me. My head on Shelby's shoulder. I sink into the darkness.

Horrible shudders yank me back to the cold and the wet and the pain. Each spasm wrenches my arm, and I gasp out sobs.

Shelby and Adam talk across me in low, panicked voices.

She says "shock" and "dangerous."

I wonder if they think it will be dangerous to brave the river or dangerous to stay. I don't really care. All my caring is wrapped up in pain and shaking and cold.

So cold. It goes all the way to the insides of my bones.

"No one knows to look for us." Adam's voice is high with fear.

I want to remind him of the siren. Maybe they are looking for us. But I can't figure out how to talk. My throat is clenched tight, and the shaking binds me.

"Rosie needs a doctor." Shelby's decided. "We have to go for it."

Adam squats down and tries to look into my face, but I'm curled into a ball and can't meet his gaze. His hand rests on my back, and I quake against it, great wrenching tremors. He says grimly, "Okay."

"B-b-but . . ." I stammer. "Only . . . Only two. Two. Two vests."

Adam pushes his hair off his forehead. "I should've brought another one. I guess I just didn't think."

"It's all right," Shelby says with fake brightness. "We'll be fine, and I'm a good swimmer."

"No one's a good swimmer in water like this," Adam protests.

"Well." Her tone is settled. "Rosie obviously has to have a life vest, and I'm not about to sacrifice my baby brother, so we'll just have to do our best to stay in the boat."

It seems like a year ago that I thought we were the life preservers. But we're not. We defeated the void, but we can't possibly defeat this river.

Shelby strides forward and starts hauling in the rope. Adam works alongside her.

I reach out vaguely, but between the shaking and the pain that comes with every movement, I'm completely useless. I stay as still as I can and wait.

Shelby holds the rope, and Adam half carries me to the boat. Some remote part of my brain registers the burning cold of the water and its insistent tug as we step into the river.

Adam bends down and cups his hands like people do when they're hoisting someone onto a horse in movies. I step into his hands and use my good arm to pull myself into the boat. Pain and nausea swirl and swirl, and I lie still, panting and waiting to feel better. The damp wood of the boat's bottom is solid and reassuring against my cheek.

Somehow Adam and Shelby get themselves into the boat, and they work the oars.

We lurch downstream. Adam grunts, and Shelby swears, but they manage to move us across the current and closer to the shore. It's like a tug of war. The current yanks us down the river, and Shelby and Adam, red-faced and straining with the effort, haul us west, over the current and closer to safety. I lie against the damp bottom of the boat and watch them handle the oars. They're doing okay, better than Adam and I did. And it helps that we have a bigger target this time.

We're not aiming for the small island. Just the riverbank. It doesn't matter if we miss the boat launch. Dry land is all that matters. And a hospital.

I use my good arm to pull myself into a sitting position. I lean, panting and shaking, against the side of the boat.

Adam jabs the water with the oars. The muscles in his neck stand out like cables.

With each stroke, Shelby grunts like a tennis player.

Beyond Adam, in the water, something approaches.

A huge, metal something. A piece of machinery. Heavy and industrial-looking. It gets closer. A bar pokes out like a hand pointing, and a chain dances madly.

I try to cry out, but my voice doesn't carry past my pain.

Adam and Shelby don't hear me. They're focused on reaching the bank. Close, but not close enough. They don't see the machine.

It travels faster than we do. It's coming.

The mottled gray and brown and black of old and rusted metal looms just over Adam's shoulder.

A scream rips out of my throat, and the pain in my arm doesn't matter, because the chain lashes wildly at the boat, and the broken piece of industry is going to kill us.

Adam follows my horrified stare and turns.

The chain whips into his face. Blood instantly sheets down from his hairline.

There's a thunderous smash and a roaring scrape, and we're in the river. The machine drags the boat away.

For a minute, Adam and I bob in the water, our orange vests holding us upright. His bangs are red with blood, which courses down the side of his face. His eyes aren't focusing.

Shelby treads water. She forces out commands between gasping breaths. "Get. To. Shore. Stay. Together."

I try for a gentle, one-armed breast stroke, but I can't move myself at all. None of us is moving, as if we're trapped in some strange whirlpool. Shelby launches herself into a strong freestyle stroke, but even though she's working hard, she stays in one spot.

Adam just hangs in the water. He raises a hand to wipe blood from his eyes.

With no warning, the current grabs me and tears me away. I don't even try to escape. It was stronger than that hideous piece of machine. It's stronger than me.

"Rosie!" Shelby's voice follows me.

The river carries me close to the shore and then tugs me back, like it's teasing me. It spins me, so now I face upstream. I can see Adam and Shelby, small and helpless, bobbing in the weird still spot. Shelby hangs on to Adam now, the two of them using his life vest to stay afloat. Maybe she is helping him stay conscious.

Water fills my mouth. I spit it out. A residue of silt coats my teeth.

Suddenly, even with the life vest, the water drags me under. I kick as hard as I can, and I'm back on the surface. I cough out river water and try to push away the pain in short, sharp breaths.

Adam and Shelby grow smaller and smaller as the river carries my body downstream.

Then the current spins me and shoves me toward a branch that hangs low, out over the water.

I can grab it. I have to grab it. I concentrate all my strength on my left arm. Hold my breath. Reach . . . and snag the branch. My fingers slip. I can't . . . but I do. I hold on. Pain races all over my body. I'm freezing and shaking, and my elbow is exploding, but I'm holding on.

Somewhere I find the strength to hoist myself up so I can hang over the branch, my good arm coiled around it. My lower legs dangle in the water, but most of me is out of the river now. I just have to hold on. And keep holding on. Until someone comes. Please, someone, come!

I whisper a pathetic, useless "Help!" but I can barely hear my own voice.

I twist as best I can to look behind me for Adam

and Shelby. The brightness of his orange vest and the glimmer of her light hair in the sunlight are all I can see.

And then the glimmer is gone. Adam's orange vest bobs alone, and a horrible wail drifts downstream.

Shelby's face bursts from the river, her mouth open, gulping air. She hurtles toward me. Her arms flail. She goes under again.

Where is she?

She surfaces. A leaf is plastered to her cheek. Her skin is pale. She's so close to me. I hear the sharp intake of breath as she struggles to fill her lungs.

I have to . . . I shift myself so I hang lower into the water. I can't hold on with my bad arm. I can't reach for her with it. I have to . . .

She's gone. A clump of leaves darts beneath me. A broken piece of Styrofoam. A . . . a wire? Headphones. It's Shelby's headphones. They swirl in a tangled mass of unnatural white beneath my dangling legs and hurry away.

I drop. My elbow explodes in new constellations of pain. I kick sharp scissor kicks, helping the vest to hold me up.

Something in the water, a tree trunk or a rock, holds me in place.

"Shelby?" I holler, somehow finding my voice.

The river races.

Shelby is nowhere.

Gone.

Into the void.

Again.

I kick something. Something solid but not.

I hold my breath. Force my head into the water. Open my eyes. But the water's too cloudy. Grainy shadows are all I see.

I kick again. This time reaching out, feeling for Shelby in the water.

She's there. Or something is.

The panic dies away, and I'm swaddled in a deliciously numb fog. Is this shock? Or hypothermia?

I think about myself like a character in a book, a character I don't really identify with in a book I don't much like.

The cold backs off. The pain in my elbow has dulled to a steady throb. Maybe I could go to sleep. Just for a few minutes.

My mind emerges from the crowding fog and shakes panic awake.

I'm not a character. I'm me, and I'm Shelby's only hope.

I extend my good arm to where I was kicking and fumble around. Something stringy and silky runs through my fingers. Hair. Shelby's long hair.

It's so silky. Soft. Like the fog. I hang in the water,

enjoying the feel of her hair floating around my hand, like sand running through your fingers at the beach. Only not warm. And not so nice. Not really. Because the hair is on a person. Shelby. A person under water. Under water too long.

Two things try to connect in my mind, but I'm floating away from myself.

Maybe I should try to pull Shelby out of the river. I should grab her hair.

I close my fist around the hair.

Maybe if I just close my eyes for a minute, I'll feel better. I snuggle into a warmth that comes from nowhere. It envelops me. It soothes away the pain in my arm.

Something orange races toward me. Adam! In a life vest . . . like mine.

He crashes into my right arm and grabs me. It's like a knife digging into my elbow, and all of a sudden, cold shoots through me, and terror snatches me from the false arms of relief. I tighten my grasp on Shelby's hair and yank.

I yank her out of the water.

She's pale. So pale. Her eyes are closed. Her lips are blue.

The three of us hang in the water. A cluster of panic and pain. Braced against the tree or rock or whatever holds us in place.

"Rope," Adam chokes out.

His eyes aren't focusing right.

I shake my head. I don't have any rope. Why would I have rope?

"Vest," he says, through chattering teeth.

Through the blood and the fear, his face steadies me. I hold on to the idea of Adam and pull myself away from oblivion.

He fumbles with his life vest. Undoes the buckles with trembling fingers.

"Hold . . . here," I whisper.

He hangs on to my vest. I hang on to Shelby, keeping her face out of the water.

Adam squirms out of his vest and unwraps the flat rope from his waist. It's not long, but the vest itself makes a sort of lasso.

He wipes blood from his eyes. Takes a breath. Tosses the vest. It collapses into the water. He tries again. The vest brushes the branch and falls away.

"You. Can. Do. This," I whisper.

He takes a breath, steadies himself against me, focuses on the branch and hurls the vest. It catches easily.

He ties the rope in his hand to my vest.

I keep hold of Shelby. I worry that I might be hurting her, pulling her around by her hair. I worry that I'm *not* hurting her. And I don't let myself think about what that means. I yank again, trying to hurt her. She is still and pale, and I hate her for not reacting to the pain. A sob rises.

"Have to work together," Adam chokes out.

I stare at the weird contraption of the life vest slung over the tree. It's like a fat, orange rope with thin strands dangling from either side. It sticks against the wet bark, but if we kick together, maybe we can shift it down the branch and move ourselves toward the bank.

I hate leaving the solidity of the thing in the water we're standing on, and I don't know if I have the strength to support myself, let alone Shelby. But we have to get out of the river. The fog hovers on the edges of my mind again, and I'm with it enough now to know the fog is oblivion. And oblivion is the end.

"On three," I whisper.

Third time's the charm. I don't say it out loud. There is no magic here.

"One," Adam grunts.

"Two," I mouth.

"Three." We say it together and shove away from our foothold. The current drags at us, but Adam hangs on to the vest-rope and hangs on to me, and I hang on to Shelby.

"Again," he commands.

On three, we kick again. It's harder because now

we're just kicking against the current, but we inch closer to the bank.

Again.

And again.

I kick, and my toes drag through the muddy bottom of the river.

"I can stand!" I cry.

We still cling to the rope and to each other, but now we stride against the current, our feet planting more and more firmly on the ground as we move out of the depth, pulling Shelby to safety.

We collapse in a pile on the leafy bank. I breathe in wet bark and rotting leaves.

Breathe. And breathe. And breathe.

Adam crawls to Shelby. Pushes her shoulder so she lies on her back.

She's so pale. Her hair lies around her head in a wet blond tangle.

I struggle toward them, but pain explodes in my elbow. My good arm and my legs are so heavy. Breathing feels like lifting weights.

Thunder rolls. A weird *chop-chop.*

Funny. Thunder in winter.

Adam puts a hand under Shelby's neck. Tips her head back. Lowers his head down to give her his breath.

One. Two. Three.

He sits back.

"Is she . . . ?" I can't finish the question.

Again, he breathes into her mouth.

Pulls away.

Her face is so still. A pale pink foam bubbles from her mouth.

How long was she under water? Not breathing. It could have been a minute, two minutes, five minutes, a year.

Something hot is on my face. I reach up and find tears.

Sobs shake me, and my elbow flames.

Adam breathes into Shelby's mouth again.

Nothing.

He roars with rage and grief. He slaps her. Her head jerks to the side.

Chop-chop-chop.

Not thunder. A helicopter.

Voices, shouting. Feet pounding on the sodden earth.

Lights.

They've come.

"Rosemary! Adam!"

"Ambulance . . ."

"Shelby," I moan.

Steady hands. A warm blanket. I let blissful nothingness swallow me.

❧

A paramedic leans over me. We jiggle and sway, and a siren screams. We must be in an ambulance.

She says "concussion." Also "shock." "Broken arm," she says to someone I can't see.

"Out of joint," I murmur.

She smiles, kind and reassuring. "Well, that's easy to fix."

The ambulance is fast and loud, like the river, but it's dry and warm, and they've already given me something that's making the pain back off.

"What about Shelby?" I ask.

Her kind smile freezes. "You'll be all right, Rosemary."

Out of joint can be fixed. *Into the void* can be fixed. But not *dead.*

Adam is lying next to me on his own stretcher. They are trying to stop the bleeding on his forehead.

We look at each other across the narrow aisle. The siren pulses.

Tears drop down onto my nose.

We stop, and the rear door flings open. They pull Adam out first, his stretcher springing into a gurney as they haul him from the ambulance. I glimpse his mother standing there, arms wrapped around herself, raw panic all over her face.

"Thank God," she moans as they roll him toward her. "Your head . . ." She reaches out, and her fingers shake as they caress his hair. "What happened? They just called me, and I came, but—"

"Where's Shelby?" he cuts in.

"I don't . . . was she with you?" She plucks at the paramedic steering Adam's stretcher. "My daughter?"

"I'm sorry, ma'am. I don't know."

They pull me out. The wheels make a high-pitched squeak as they rush me toward the door.

"Rosemary?" Mrs. Steiner is hurrying alongside. "Was Shelby with you?"

We pause at a desk, and she leans over me.

"Do you know where Shelby is?"

My voice comes out in a whisper. "We found her, but . . ."

I can't say the next words.

Mrs. Steiner's face crumples. My heart breaks.

Nineteen

I STRUGGLE THROUGH THE FOG of anesthesia into consciousness. There's a dull throb in my elbow, but the stabbing, breathtaking pain is gone. A splint cradles my arm, and a tidy blue sling rests against my chest. I'm warm and dry.

Mom's sitting beside me, a book unopened on her lap.

"Adam?" I croak.

She leans forward and rests her hand on my cheek, the way she did when I was little and had a fever.

"He'll be fine." Her voice is low, cradling me in its calm. "He has a concussion, fifteen stitches, but he's all right."

She sets her book aside.

I steel myself. She will tell me now that Shelby is dead. My fingertips and my kneecaps are numb, already crushed under the weight of the grief that's coming. Stabbing grief and rushing guilt.

Mom won't know it, but I'll know and Adam will know that it's our fault Shelby is dead. We rescued her from one void only to send her into a different one.

"Shel . . ." I whisper, because I don't have enough air to say her name.

Mom looks down at her hands. "They took her by helicopter to the medical center in Lionville."

Dead people don't get taken to medical centers.

"They don't know how long she was unconscious," Mom continues. "She nearly drowned. You all nearly . . ." The words choke off.

Adam and I didn't drown. We held on. To the branch. To each other.

But not to Shelby. Her hair floats through my fingers. Horrible pink foam bubbles slowly from her blue lips.

I force out the question. "Will she live?"

Mom doesn't look at me. Her hands clutched in her lap tell me that she doesn't know.

I turn onto my side and curl my knees to my chest.

Mom's voice is far away. Broken and garbled.

" . . . brain function . . . medically induced coma . . ."

Void and nothing. Void and nothing. Void and nothing.

To void and nothing, turn life.

The one-legged Barbie grins crookedly. Shelby's headphones disappear.

The poem won after all.

I must have fallen asleep. I don't know how much time has passed.

"Rosie." Mom sets down her book when she sees I'm awake. "How do you feel?"

"Sleepy." I stretch.

"It's the pain medicine," Mom says. "And the trauma."

Her hand on my cheek again. I raise my good arm and press my hand on top of hers.

She makes a small, strangled sound. She's crying. "Oh, Rosie. I love you so much. I don't know what I'd do . . . if I ever . . . if you ever . . ." Her head drops on to the side of my bed.

I try to stroke her hair the way she does mine, but I'm clumsy with my left hand, and all I manage is an awkward pat.

A hand reaches into my chest and twists my heart. She's so emotional because Shelby's . . . because Shelby . . .

"Is Shelby . . . ?" a voice asks. My voice. I ask.

Mom shakes her head. "There's no change."

She's still alive.

Mom grasps my hand. "Don't you *ever* . . ." she begins.

"I'm sorry, Mom."

I'm sorry I wrote in Shakespeare's book. I'm sorry I said magic words out loud. I'm sorry I went to the island. I'm sorry I didn't think about life preservers. I'm sorry I didn't hold on to Shelby.

"I'm sorry," I whisper, but no one cares that I'm sorry. Sorry doesn't make any difference.

Mom squeezes my hand too tight. My knuckles grind against each other. It hurts, but it's the opposite of dislocated. She assures herself I'm here. She assures me she's here.

I look right into her red-rimmed eyes. "I love you."

"I know." She smiles through the fury and the relief. "I love you too."

"When can I leave here? Can we go to Lionville and see Shelby?"

Mom manages to hold her voice steady. "She's still in a coma. They've brought her body temperature back to normal, which is good . . ." She hesitates, then says, "They're running some tests on her brain."

"What for?"

She sighs. "To determine if she's suffered any brain damage."

I go cold. Not brain damage. Not Shelby.

Brain damage and Constance is bad enough. She gazes out at the falling snow. She gives me a vacant smile. She stretches her arm out toward the candy dish. She asks, "Do I know you?"

It's too late for Constance. The damage is done. But not Shelby. Please, not Shelby.

"We just have to wait now." Mom rests her hand lightly on my good arm.

We have to wait to see if Shelby's brain is in the void.

"Where's Adam?" I whisper.

"He's here. In the hospital. They kept him overnight for observation, but he'll be discharged today. You both will."

"It's tomorrow?" I frown.

She smiles, a tired, tight smile. "As Macbeth says, 'Tomorrow and tomorrow and—'"

"Don't." I cut her off. "Just . . . don't."

When I surface from an uneasy sleep, Mom's texting.

"Shelby?" I ask.

"No news. I'm sorry."

"Who're you texting?"

"Your father," she answers as she returns the phone to her bag.

"Why?"

She shrugs. "I thought he should know what's going on."

It makes sense that she would tell him when something major happens to me, or because of me. I try to imagine him caring, but I can't. He forgot about us so long ago that I can't possibly be more than a nagging memory at the edge of his life.

"What did he say?" I ask.

"He's glad you're all right," she says.

"That's all?"

"That's all."

I'm just one more book he started to read and then left behind, unfinished. He doesn't miss me, which is fine. I don't miss him, either. How could I? I don't even know him. But Mom . . . they were married. They had a kid.

"Do you miss him?" I ask.

She answers slowly. "I miss the idea of what he was a long time ago, when we were younger and he seemed so easygoing, willing to let me shape our lives. It seemed generous, and I was grateful. And he is a good person . . . but do I miss him now? No, I don't. The void he left in my life was filled up long ago with my work and my friends and my daughter." She smiles at me.

But her smile is a knife in my heart. What if Shelby leaves us? If she dies or if her brain dies, what will ever fill the void?

Tears come, and sobs rip upward from my gut.

Mom holds me and loves me, but she can't help Shelby.

I collapse into hiccups, and Mom lays me back against the pillows. Her hand rests on my cheek again.

A light tap, and Adam pushes open the door. A line of Frankenstein stitches jags across his forehead.

I sit up. "Are you okay?"

"Fine." He runs his fingertips over the stitches and lets out a breath, like he's been holding it since we were in the river. "I'm fine, and so's Shelby."

"She's fine?" I don't trust the words.

"Her brain is fine," he says.

His eyes are full of tears. "She's still in a coma, but it's, like, artificial. I mean, they put her in it, so her body could focus on basic stuff. Like being alive." He grins at me, looking a little crazy and a lot relieved. "My dad said he'd drive us to Lionville. So we can see her." He looks at Mom. "If Rosie's ready to check out."

"She's supposed to be discharged this morning," Mom answers. "I'll try to hurry them along."

She presses the red call button, and a nurse bustles into the room.

We have to wait for them to pull out my IV, and a different nurse has to check my vital signs one more time. Mom goes off with an administration person to do paperwork. It doesn't seem like we'll ever be able to leave.

Adam and I alternate between uneasy smiles and somber stares. Sometimes he looks away. Sometimes I do. Neither of us can face what happened head-on. Not yet.

Finally, we load our battered bodies into the back of Mr. Steiner's car. Adam has to buckle my seat belt because I can't do it one handed.

"We're a mess," I observe, but I'm grinning as he reaches across me.

He looks up, his face close to mine. A black thread sticks out through his bangs. I feel an urge to pull it, to unravel everything that's happened over the past two weeks.

We ride in a silence thick with all the questions Mom and Mr. Steiner must want to ask, but no one says anything. The countryside flashes past. And the river flows south. It carries silt and branches and broken bits and maybe Barbie.

But not us.

Adam and Shelby and I survived.

Lionville is all sterile corridors and bright lights. Nurses and doctors stride past us as Mom and I wait for the Steiners to come back from wherever the doctor took them.

My elbow throbs faintly, and an ache presses between my eyes.

"I brought you these." Mom opens her bag to show a handful of my books. "I had them when you were in Cookfield Hospital, but you weren't awake long enough to read. Maybe now? To pass the time? They were the ones nearest your bed, so I thought they'd be the ones you'd want."

Pelagia's Boats, with its battered spine, is sandwiched between two other books, almost as worn.

Tears fill my eyes. I can't quite see the book, but my fingers recognize the feel of it. I pull it from the bag and clutch it against me.

Finally, the Steiners come through a swinging door. Only three of them, but everyone knows now that there are really four. I'm sure their kitchen table is scooted out from the wall.

Mrs. Steiner gives me a big hug. "I'm so glad you're all right," she murmurs into my hair.

I can't speak. I nearly killed her daughter.

When she releases me, the back cover drops off my book.

Mr. Steiner bends to pick it up. "This is one of Shelby's favorites," he says with a sort of numb surprise.

Mrs. Steiner tells us, "The doctor says she'll probably suffer some memory loss, and she may have trouble with disturbances to her vision for a little while, but they think she will be okay."

"Her brain will be okay," Adam adds.

"It seems she was not unconscious for long," Mr. Steiner says. "You two pulled her from the water in time."

Adam and I lean into each other. I'm sure we're thinking the same thing: She was only in the water because of us.

"Can we see her?" Adam asks.

"They say only family—" Mr. Steiner begins.

"Rosemary is family," Adam protests, and no one argues.

We enter a dim room. A machine attached to Shelby beeps, a steady, regular beat. Her color is normal, almost. Someone brushed her hair, and it fans out neatly behind her head. Her eyes are closed. She could be sleeping. Her chest rises slightly. And falls.

I shove away the memory of Adam trying to give her mouth-to-mouth, trying to help her breathe. I focus on now.

Shelby is lying in front of me, alive.

She is here.

We pulled her out of the void.

After a long moment, Mom suggests, "Why don't you read to her?"

"She'd like that," Mr. Steiner says.

"Can she hear us?" Adam asks.

"They don't know," Mrs. Steiner answers. "But if she can, listening to you two read her favorite book would be nice for her."

So Adam and I sit together in chairs drawn up close

to the bed. My knees bump into the metal frame. I hold the book open in my lap.

Tears swim in my eyes again, but I know how the book begins. I say the words from memory.

Epilogue

WHEN THEY WAKE SHELBY, Mr. and Mrs. Steiner report she remembers nothing from that day, but her brain is working fine. The doctors say over and over how lucky she is, how lucky all of us are.

She'll want us to fill in the gaps in her memory eventually, but for now, she's content to just hang out. We tell her that we read her *Pelagia's Boats* while she was in a coma. We talk about everything and nothing, and it's like it used to be, except we're all older now. Pam and Maria and John come visit, and some of the other kids from the musical, and two of Shelby's teachers. And even Mr. Cates.

I realize for the first time how wonderful it is that Adam and I aren't the only people who love Shelby. Having friends and being busy after school means she's *here.* And Shelby's worth sharing.

When she's well enough, we take her to see Constance. We all wear the slim silver bracelets we had made at a kiosk in the mall. A computer etched the words onto the silver: *Rosemary, that's for remembrance. Pray, love, remember.*

We talked about getting one for Constance, too, but we decided not to burden her with the memory of Wilkie's loss. The rhyme can only cause her pain, but it keeps Wilkie alive in our memories, at least a little. Maybe when Constance and her mangled memory die, Wilkie will slip away, but for now, we hold on to him. And that's not nothing.

For Constance, the void poem isn't the real enemy now. It's the Alzheimer's. We brought the little book of her poems and a huge stack of library books, and I think every poem she wrote is with us in the room. Maybe all these rhymes will remind her of her own long life.

It was Shakespeare who gave me the idea. He says *you live in this.* The poem is *a living record of your memory,* and Constance wrote lots of poems. She may have forgotten her own life, most of it, but it lives in these books, in the words she wrote.

"Constance?" I call to her.

She turns her head and smiles, that soft, gentle smile. "Hello. Do I . . . ? I think I know you. Don't I?"

"This is Adam. I'm Rosemary. And this is Michelle."

Shelby puts an arm around me and murmurs, "Shelby's fine."

"Rosemary," Constance echoes. "Father always says he could grow rosemary at the North Pole, if given the chance, and I think he could. Do you know he planted rosemary in our garden? On the island?"

"Constance," I say. "We brought you your poems."

"Poems?" she repeats. "I won the recitation prize in the third grade for that lovely Wordsworth poem about the daffodils. Shall I say it?"

She recites:

> I wandered lonely as a cloud
> That floats on high o'er vales and hills,

She pauses but this time she continues, with confidence in her voice:

> When all at once I saw a crowd,
> A host, of golden daffodils;

She hits the stressed syllables with a cadence her body knows even though her mind has lost so much. I wonder what I'll remember when I'm old and my memory fails. I'll be lucky if I hang on to a poem, like Constance has.

> They flash upon that inward eye
> Which is the bliss of solitude;

And then my heart with pleasure fills,
And dances with the daffodils.

The words dance in the room, a miracle of memory.

"How . . . ?" Adam begins.

"She can remember it because she knew it when she was young," I whisper. "That part of her is still there. That's why she remembered the void poem."

"This one's about memory too," Shelby says. "Wordsworth remembers the daffodils."

Constance nods. "*They flash upon that inward eye.*"

"You have the poem in your inward eye," I tell her.

She laughs, a soft, wispy sound. It wafts away, as her focus fades.

We read her a few of her own poems, and she listens. Maybe she remembers.

When we finally finished our poetry project, we printed it on crisp white paper, bound it in a bright rainbow-striped folder, and handed it in to Mr. Cates.

We didn't use the codex. It had to be someplace safe. Not to protect the book from harm, but to protect the people who might read it.

So we locked it up. In the cupboard in my room where Constance had hidden it.

I used pliers to twist the metal J of the hidden release back on itself. I made it impossible for anyone to open the door.

Adam tested it.

I pried at it with a crowbar.

Shelby tried "Open Sesame," and she made it sound like a joke, but it wasn't really, because we know now that magic words are real.

The door wouldn't budge.

The cupboard is shut. Forever, I hope.

When we got our project back from Mr. Cates, he told us he loved it and said we'd definitely found our muse.

Today we're giving it to Constance.

"This is for you," I say. I set the binder on her night table next to the candy dish, filled with new peppermints in shiny wrappers.

"It's poems," Adam explains. "Some of yours and some we wrote, kind of inspired by yours. By you."

She smiles. "Thank you."

"You were our muse." I say the words lightly, but they're true.

As we leave the room, she reaches for the binder, another living record.

We follow the corridor past Jonas, the man who misses his wife, Maud.

"It's not fair that she doesn't get Wilkie back," I

say. "And Wilkie gets nothing. He didn't get to live his life or to write poems or make art or leave anything behind."

"There are all kinds of loss," Shelby muses. "Didn't Constance's mom die when she was young? She doesn't get her mom back, either."

"And I don't get my dad," I say.

There is loss in life, and the best we can do is face it head on and meet it with grace and remembrance.

I walk with Adam and Shelby out into warming air, and it strikes me that growing older is like the V tree. It has a solid foundation, but it branches out, strong arms reaching up and away.

Thanks

Thank you to the many wise people who read versions of this book and helped me see how to be a better writer, especially Jordan Sonnenblick, Joe Scapellato, Debbie Ware, Jo Fleming, Elisabeth Guerrero, Ghislaine McDayter, Shelby Radcliffe, Dave Kristjanson-Gural, and Robert Rosenberg. Very special thanks to Pam Brunskill and Maria Hebert-Leiter, my wonderful critique partners, for careful reading, keen insight, and enthusiasm.

Thank you to the late George Nicholson for believing in my writing.

Thank you to Dinah Stevenson for knowing when less is more.

Thank you to Pa and SM for a lifetime of unwavering support, to Jordi for being my best advocate, and to Elijah, Aley, and Thea—my muses—for listening and love.

Most of all, thank you to Kristen, for being my best friend since third grade and for always knowing what I should read next.

Rosemary's Bookshelf

ALICE'S ADVENTURES IN WONDERLAND
by Lewis Carroll (1865)

Some people consider this the first book written for the purpose of entertaining children, as opposed to teaching them lessons of one kind or another. Alice falls down a rabbit hole into a nonsensical world where reality is comically and a little uncomfortably altered.

CORALINE
by Neil Gaiman (2002)

Gaiman tells the story of a girl who discovers a mirror world behind a door in her living room. The other house she finds there is like her house but with some chilling differences. The other parents are eager to keep Coraline in their world. Careful readers might notice that *Coraline* is, in some ways, a retelling of *Alice's Adventures in Wonderland*.

THE GIVER
by Lois Lowry (1993)

Set in a dystopian future that values sameness, *The Giver* is about the vital role of memory in society. As he turns twelve, Jonas comes to recognize the ways in which his community suffers because people have turned away from difference and from the lessons of the past.

THE GOLDEN COMPASS
by Philip Pullman (1995)

The first book in Pullman's *His Dark Materials* trilogy was published in the UK as *Northern Lights.* It tells the story of a brave young girl destined to play a central role in a battle that will change the world. Lyra is exceptionally gifted at telling stories and has a special ability to read the truth.

HARRY POTTER AND THE CHAMBER OF SECRETS
by J. K. Rowling (1998)

In the second book in the famous Harry Potter series, Harry finds an old diary that reveals secret information about Hogwarts. When Harry writes in the book, the book seems to write back.

SEVEN-DAY MAGIC
by Edward Eager (1962)

Five children find a mysterious old book in the library. The book can be checked out for only seven days, but in that time, it creates magical adventures for its readers.

THE STORY OF THE AMULET
by E. Nesbit (1906)

This is the final book in a trilogy that features a family of children who have a series of magical adventures. They find an ancient Egyptian amulet that allows them to travel in time.

WHEN YOU REACH ME

by Rebecca Stead (2009)

In this novel, set in 1979, the main character uses her favorite book, *A Wrinkle in Time,* to make sense of confusing events in her life. Her best friend is ignoring her, her relationship with her mom is changing, and she receives a series of mysterious notes from a person who seems able to predict the future.

A WRINKLE IN TIME

by Madeleine L'Engle (1962)

Twelve-year-old Meg Murry journeys across space-time to rescue her father from imprisonment on a distant planet. She relies on her friend and her younger brother, but most of all, she relies on her own faults.

PELAGIA'S BOATS

by Virginia Zimmerman (date unknown)

This book doesn't exist yet, though I intend to write it someday. It will be based on a story I used to tell my children, featuring a heroine called Pelagia who saves the people of her dying island home.